A Candlelight Ecstasy Romance ®

FOR A MOMENT HER GAZE FUSED WITH HIS—SIMMERING, MELTING, BURNING . . .

And then, with a catch of her breath, she came forward and her lips met his in a blaze of heat. They both moaned with pleasure as they deepened the kiss. Her fingers plundered the softness of his hair as his hands roved along her back, over her hips, and then found the heat of her skin under her shirt. The touch was incredibly exciting, igniting her senses and dissolving her protests.

"I think," he whispered, his breath warm against her lips, "I think we were meant for this a long, long time ago. And that's why it's silly," he whispered, "to pretend it isn't true."

A CANDLELIGHT ECSTASY ROMANCE ®

WITH EVERY LOVING TOUCH

Nell Kincaid

Candlelight Ecstasy Romance ®

is a trademark of Dell Publishing Co., Inc.,
New York, New York

A CANDLELIGHT ECSTASY ROMANCE ®

Published by
Dell Publishing Co., Inc.
1 Dag Hammarskjold Plaza
New York, New York 10017

Dell ® TM 681510, Dell Publishing Co., Inc.

Candlelight Ecstasy Romance®, 1,203,540, is a registered
trademark of Dell Publishing Co., Inc.,
New York, New York.

ISBN: 0-440-19661-2

Printed in the United States of America
First printing—June 1983

To Our Readers:

We have been delighted with your enthusiastic response to Candlelight Ecstasy Romances®, and we thank you for the interest you have shown in this exciting series.

In the upcoming months, we will continue to present the distinctive sensuous love stories you have come to expect only from Ecstasy. We look forward to bringing you many more books from your favorite authors and also the very finest work from new authors of contemporary romantic fiction.

As always, we are striving to present the unique, absorbing love stories that you enjoy most—books that are more than ordinary romance.

Your suggestions and comments are always welcome. Please write to us at the address below.

Sincerely,

The Editors
Candlelight Romances
1 Dag Hammarskjold Plaza
New York, New York 10017

CHAPTER ONE

Marina Tolchin stepped out of the elevator and walked over to the receptionist at a large desk under the words "Taft, Wilshire, and Honeywell, Attorneys-at-Law."

Marina introduced herself, and the receptionist smiled and asked her to have a seat. Marina sat on a large leather couch and looked around at the plush surroundings—smoked-glass doors, luxurious thick carpeting, fine paintings—all furnishings only a solid and conservative corporate law practice could afford.

The day was a bittersweet one, made of both pleasure and pain, for while she would be seeing Dan Sommers after nearly a year, the occasion was a sad one: the reading of her grandmother's will, with the last handful of the Tolchins meagerly present.

Marina tried to think of something more cheerful; after all, her family for years had consisted only of her, her brother Alex, her grandmother Tatiana, and her great-aunt and great-uncle. And for years she had known this day would come, when her family would be nearly gone—almost eighty years after her grandparents and their brothers and sisters had first come from Russia to America.

At least she was firmly settled and relatively happy, having weathered a rocky marriage and divorce by age twenty-five and several career changes since college. Now, at age thirty, she felt for the first time in her life as if she knew what she wanted. She had recently—just two weeks before, in fact—met a man she really liked, someone she had been introduced to at a party out in Sag Harbor. Barclay was easygoing and intelligent, a writer who had been living in the city for just a few months. And she felt, for the first time since her divorce, as if she had met someone she might be able to have a good, solid, and exciting relationship with. And she had just been made head chef at one of New York City's most popular *cuisine minceur* restaurants, which made her one of the only two female French chefs in the city. Though it had been a backbreaking struggle to become even a sous chef, and though people had looked down on her at the beginning, when she had been a prep woman in the kitchen of a completely obscure little restaurant, she knew now she had made the right choices. True, friends of hers from college who had become doctors, lawyers, architects had raised their eyebrows when she had said she was a prep woman; but she learned then that they weren't really her friends, that they couldn't be if they judged someone on those terms.

She had learned then how important it was to follow one's instincts, no matter what people thought. And today she'd follow her instincts, whatever was in store for her. Her grandmother had not been well-off financially over the past several years, but the woman had always had a lively and mischievous imagination; and Marina suspected that Tatiana had made her will interesting if nothing else.

A door to the inner offices of Taft, Wilshire, and Honeywell opened, and a pretty young woman was soon leading Marina down a quiet hallway to Dan Sommers's office. "Mr. Sommers had to step out for a moment, Miss Tolchin. But you can wait in his office if you'd like. You're expecting others, aren't you?"

"I think so," Marina said, certain that her brother had been summoned, perhaps along with her great-aunt and great-uncle. Though whether her brother would show up, Marina had no idea.

A few moments later she was alone in Dan's office. It was a lovely room, with richly hued Oriental rugs, Impressionist paintings, and antique walnut and oak furniture. But it was not what she would have guessed for Dan Sommers—at least not for the Dan she had known in college. He had been such an outdoorsman back then, a young man from Wisconsin in the foothills of Vermont, a man who had taken advantage of the sylvan setting of their college at every opportunity—mountain-climbing, skiing, hiking. He had been a spirited idealist back then as well, fighting for everything from the rights of animals on campus to world issues he believed in. And now he was an attorney for some of the very corporations he had opposed, working on cases that were more concerned with money than with the causes he had once espoused so fervently.

After college, when he had married Marina's friend Ellie, he had changed almost overnight, becoming desperately ambitious and shedding his former personality as if it had never existed. Marina had neither liked nor understood what she saw, and her friendship with first Dan and then Ellie had gradually faded.

What had happened to Dan had happened to her ex-husband, too, though with Rick there had been many additional problems. But the breaking point had come when Rick had refused to "let" her begin her cooking career because it would interfere with his. He had actually used the word "let," saying it wouldn't work—though he never explained what her working or not working had to do with his job as an advertising manager for a large department store in New York. Marina didn't know whether Dan had taken a similar stance with Ellie; perhaps he hadn't needed to, as she had never intended to have a job. All Marina knew was that she was sorry Dan had changed so much over the years, and in ways so similar to Rick.

Dan and Ellie had separated a year ago, and the only time Marina had seen him since was once, by accident, at a restaurant where she had been with a date. Dan had come in after she and her date were already seated. He was with a tall, model-pretty blonde—a woman who at a glance was obviously the opposite of Ellie; and as fate would have it, the two couples had had to sit next to each other. Dan and Marina had said polite, even warm, hellos, introducing everyone all around, and then an awkwardness had descended as they all realized they would be within very close earshot of each other for the entire evening. Marina, on her second date with her companion, felt uncomfortable from the moment Dan and his date finally sat down and Dan had turned his back to her. But she had felt twice as uncomfortable when Dan began talking. And she was suddenly depressed as well: for she had had to listen to Dan—the new Dan—try to impress his date with all the qualities he had so recently acquired: zealous ambition, knowledge of everything that was current and trendy, even a perhaps exaggerated appreciation of the joys of bachelorhood. Marina knew she couldn't put too much credence in what he was saying: he was obviously on his first date with the woman, he was nervous, and apparently trying his best to impress her. But somehow the very fact that he wasn't being totally honest—just as she sometimes hedged with her dates—had made the situation all the more depressing: he sounded like dozens of men she had met at bars before she had realized there was simply no point in going. And she saw that if she had never known Dan in college and had been sitting where his date now was, she wouldn't have liked him much. No, she wouldn't have liked him much at all.

But there was no use dwelling on the past. Seeing

Dan after all this time would have to be nicer than it had been at the restaurant; at the very least they would both be more relaxed.

Marina stood up and walked to the large picture window behind Dan's desk. The view was magnificent, with all of midtown Manhattan visible—solid, gray, endless.

Behind her the door opened, and she turned.

There stood Dan, framed in the doorway, dark and tanned, athletic-looking even in his very conservative gray suit. His eyes were the same rich dark brown, his hair the same luxuriant chestnut. And he was smiling his wonderful easy smile, relaxed and totally sincere. Marina felt in an instant as if all the years since college had never even passed.

"Marina," he said softly and then came forward, as did she, to embrace.

They put their arms around each other and kissed on the cheek, then drew back to look at each other.

"You look fantastic," he said, smiling.

"So do you," she said.

Suddenly they were both aware that they were still holding each other, his arms at her waist and her hands on his arms. They looked into each other's eyes and gently broke the embrace. Then he smiled, his warm brown eyes sparkling. "It's so good to see you," he said. "I've been thinking about you a lot lately, with Tatiana's will and all. I'm sorry we ever fell out of touch, Marina."

"Yes, well, things weren't really the same . . . after college," she said. She hadn't been able to say "after we were both married," for that would have distorted her meaning. She and Dan had not been victims of fate or poor choice, wildly attracted to each other but married to others; they had simply been good friends. But their friendship wasn't the type to adapt to marriage; it had been deep and private, made up of only the two of them and no one else. True, they had often been together in a group, but the good moments, the valuable ones, had been between the two of them: taking long walks in the woods, discussing everything from politics to problems they were having on dates; studying together all night and then driving around at 4:00 A.M. on mad hunts for food; and sharing their most painful moments, too. In Marina's sophomore year, when her parents had been killed in a freak boating accident, she had gone not to her then-boyfriend but to Dan—the only person in the world she had wanted to be with. He had held her in his arms, and she had cried, and then he had driven her to the city, staying with her until she was ready to have him leave, making everything infinitely less painful.

Everyone—including Dan and Marina themselves —had wondered why, if they were such good friends, they didn't go out together. They had laughed about it—nervously, not knowing quite what to think. Marina had said she didn't want to ruin what they had, to complicate such an uncomplicated relationship: if they were friends, the friendship would never have to end; while if they went out together, the relationship would inevitably end, as more intimate relationships always did and perhaps always would.

15

As it stood, it was safe and wonderful: they could talk about anything.

But now, seeing Dan alone for the first time in ages, she wondered how she had found it so easy to be merely friends with him back in college. Everything about him—his dark attractiveness, his affectionate voice, his eyes that so clearly appreciated her—was unsettling and made her feel awkward, almost as if she were meeting him for the first time.

"I'm, uh, sorry, Marina, that we had to get together because of Tatiana's death—" When she looked into his eyes, they were intensely sad. "You know, I knew her pretty well."

Marina nodded. "I can remember the day she first met you, at my parents' house." She laughed. "After you left, Tati raved about you for hours and said if she couldn't have you as a son-in-law, at least you could be her lawyer."

A flash of sadness shot through his eyes, but then he half-smiled. "She was the last private client I took on," he mused, "before I began with all this." He gestured around at the office.

The intercom on his desk buzzed, and he went and picked up the phone.

Marina watched as he said, "Yes, send him in, please," and gave some other instructions to his secretary. He was handsomer than he had been in college; though he had been older than almost everyone else there, having been in the army first, he had still seemed not quite a man back then—still part boy, young and slim. But now he had reached a wonderful age, a perfect weight and shape for his frame. His jaw was a bit fuller, his shoulders broader, yet he looked as powerful as ever.

He replaced the receiver and said, "Your brother's coming in," his expression cryptically apprehensive.

"What's the matter?" Marina asked.

He sighed, his dark brown eyes hesitant. "I spoke with him last week," he began, "and . . . well, let's just say he wasn't too keen on coming in unless he knew what—"

The door opened and Dan's secretary stepped in, followed by Marina's brother Alex.

He hardly looked at Marina, his dark blue eyes concentrating instead on Dan. "Well, I'm here," he said sullenly.

"I'm glad you could come," Dan said, ignoring Alex's rudeness. "It's nice to meet you after all this time. You two look amazingly alike."

For a moment Marina thought she could see the hint of a smile behind Alex's hostile mask. They did look alike, and the resemblance was all the more apparent because they were both rather exotic-looking, with high cheekbones; pale blue, almost slanted, eyes; jet-black hair; and full, dark lips. The two were male and female versions of each other, often mistaken for twins, but Alex was saved from prettiness by a slightly crooked nose and rough, apparently never-shaven skin.

"Well," Dan said. "We might as well get started. I told your great-aunt and -uncle not to come unless they absolutely wanted to, since it's so hard for them to travel and the bulk of the estate, as you'll soon see, goes to the two of you."

Alex raised a brow. "Then let's get to it," he said, pulling up a chair to Dan's desk and sitting down.

"Why don't you relax, Alex?" Marina said with annoyance. "Try thinking about whom this is coming from. And why."

Alex rolled his eyes and looked at Dan. "You'll have to forgive my sister, Mr. Sommers. She has a streak of sentimentality as wide as Texas. And a streak of sanctimoniousness that rivals it."

"Alex!" Marina protested.

"I rather think you're the one I'll have to try to forgive, Alex," Dan said as he sat down behind his desk. "And Marina wasn't the only person in this room who loved your grandmother. I loved her, too."

Alex blinked and shook his head. "Uh-uh. You misunderstand me," he said. "I'm not talking about my grandmother. I loved her as much as anybody. More. I'm talking about my sister here, who thinks you can't smile for two weeks after someone dies." His voice was low and quavering, almost breaking with tension. He looked into Marina's eyes for the first time since he had come in, and Marina suddenly wanted to cry; he looked so sad, so full of pain, and she knew he was fighting emotions he thought made him weak, feelings he thought were wrong.

Dan's voice broke the long gaze. "I think it would be best if I just read the will," he said. "You'll both have a lot to talk about afterward."

Marina looked questioningly at Dan, but he merely set out a blue-bound sheaf of papers on the desk. And then he began to read. "I, Tatiana Alexeva, residing in the City of New York, State of New York, do hereby make, publish, and declare this to be my last will and testament, hereby revoking any and all former wills and codicils by me at any time heretofore made. First: Though Marina and Alex don't know about this, I never sold Windy Hill, the inn we owned for many, many years up in the Shawangunk Mountains."

Shocked, Marina glanced at Alex, but he was looking fixedly at Dan, waiting for him to continue. Dan cleared his throat and went on. "I remember the summers when Marina and Alex played so happily. They fought like cats and dogs, but they made up easily. Now it is different and they don't make up at all. Many years ago I was going to sell Windy Hill. I needed the money, and I could no longer run it. But then Marina and Alex were alone after their parents died, and I knew I could never sell Windy Hill. We would have no history in the family, and soon we would have no memories. Now Windy Hill is all I have, except for a few possessions not worth very much except to me. I leave Windy Hill to you, Marina and Alex. Naturally I want to see you bring it back to life. But do that only if it will make you happy. Otherwise sell it and enjoy the money. My only proviso (thank you, my Dan, for the word) is that neither one of you may sell his or her share without the permission of the other. This is something you two will do together. And you will stop fighting one of these days, I know. I want to help. And I'll always love you."

Dan put down the papers and looked into Marina's eyes. "I'll, uh, read the rest now," he said quietly, and he read the small amount that was left of the will. Tatiana had left the bulk of her remaining possessions—some furniture and clothes—to her brother and sister. And she had left several photograph albums and memoirs she had written in her childish, earnest script to Marina and Alex, with one special one for Marina. "I want you to pass along to your children, Alex and Marina, the tales of our family coming over from Russia," she had written. "Someday you will see how important this is. But these are only memories, my grandchildren. Most of all I would like you to concentrate on Windy Hill. Work with it. Make something of it if you can. If not, then that's the course you choose. All I want is for the two of you to love each other. I will love you forever."

Dan leaned back in his chair, and there were a few moments of silence. Then he sighed and spoke. "When she wrote this," he said, "she thought it was very subtle." He smiled. "I remember her saying, 'I don't want them to feel under pressure. Am I pressuring them, Danny? Tell me and I'll change it.' She reworked it again and again and again, and each time it came out the same. She wanted you to keep Windy Hill. Finally we left it that way; we both felt it was important that you know what she wanted, although she's leaving it up to you. Anyway, we had a lot of fun with it because she tried rewriting it so many times and it always came out 'just not perfect,' as she kept saying. But it *was* good enough."

Marina smiled, but when she looked at Alex, his

20

face was stretched taut with anger. "That's just great," he said. "You sit behind that big desk of yours and say you laughed. You *could* laugh. But what are *we* left with?"

Dan looked puzzled. "You're left with Windy Hill, of course. Or cash. Whichever you like."

Alex glared at him. "We're also left with a load of guilt," he said, his voice hoarsely aggressive. "And I know what you're thinking. You're thinking we shouldn't sell because she was a great woman and we shouldn't go against her wishes. Well, I have news for you. No matter how well off you think I am running that ad agency, forget it. The company's tiny, business is rotten, and the money from Windy Hill is money I could use."

Dan frowned. "Now *you* misunderstand *me*, Mr. Tolchin. I told Tatiana, and I'll tell you now. My advice is to sell. And Tatiana knew I'd advise that."

Marina stared. "Are you serious?" she asked, her voice nearly a whisper. The two men looked at her, their expressions unreadable. "I can't believe what I'm hearing. We all heard the same thing—Tati's sincere wish that we keep Windy Hill and try to make a go of it—and Dan, you obviously discussed it with her pretty thoroughly. But without even hesitating, you both recommend selling."

Dan sighed. "I certainly haven't agreed with everything your brother has said today, Marina. But there's one thing I can't argue with. People have to make a living, and sometimes they have to make decisions that are unsentimental and very difficult. But I don't even see any question here. Keeping

Windy Hill would run you into the ground financially almost immediately. Unless the two of you wanted to keep it as a summer house."

"Are you kidding?" Alex said. "Forget it. If I had a summer house, it wouldn't be a share with my sister, and it certainly wouldn't be in upstate New York. The Hamptons or Fire Island, maybe. But upstate? Forget it."

Marina sighed and shook her head. "I really can't believe you. Either of you. But especially you, Alex," she said, turning to her brother. "Don't you realize we're alone now? It's just the two of us. Do you really want that? Do you really want to be cut off with nothing to remember anybody by?"

Alex frowned. "Of course not, Marina. That isn't the point. The point is that you don't hold onto a memory when it costs that much—"

"And you don't let go when it costs that much emotionally," she cut in. "Alex, I'm not saying we have to keep it. I don't even know how we would. I'm just saying that we should at least go up to see it and then think about what we want to do."

She turned to Dan. "You ought to at least agree to *that,* Dan. All lawyers ever say is 'I'll get back to you,' and 'You should consider the possibilities carefully.' So why not now?"

Dan shrugged. "Sounds good to me."

She shot him a baleful look. "Then you should have suggested that to begin with," she said. "Really. It was very irresponsible not to."

He half-smiled. "I think the two of you can take care of yourselves, Marina. And you'll do what you

22

want no matter what I say. I just gave you my advice —something Tatiana expected me to do."

She sighed, looking into his eyes. Of course he had the right to give his advice; people paid him to do that. But it all seemed so mercenary, so cut and dried. "I guess Alex and I will have to talk about it," she said. "And we'll let you know."

"You'll get back to me, in lawyers' parlance?" She smiled. "Why don't you stay?" he asked softly. "Just for a bit."

She glanced at Alex, who still looked annoyed. "Alex, I'll call you, then, *after* I've seen Windy Hill. In a few days."

"Sure," he said, standing up. "We don't have anything to talk about—there's nothing to discuss. But call if you want."

"Alex, you seem to forget. You may not want to discuss any of this, but unless you get my consent, you can't sell."

He frowned. "We'll see about that," he said quietly, and after saying a curt good-bye to Dan, he left the office.

As soon as Alex was gone, Dan came around to the front of the desk and sat on the edge, in front of Marina. "I'm sorry it didn't go that well," he said, "and I'm sorry I made that recommendation, Marina. It just seemed—"

"It doesn't matter," she said quietly, looking up at him. "It had nothing to do with you, and I'm sure it would have gone worse if someone other than you had been here."

There was a silence, and suddenly they were looking at each other differently, eyes meeting each other's and seeing someone altogether new. They had been so much younger when they had been friends all those years ago, and Marina was unused to the sensation of looking at her friend Dan and seeing, instead, an extremely attractive man. She smiled uneasily. "This is a little odd, isn't it—meeting like this after all this time, after so many things have happened."

He pursed his lips, gazing at her speculatively. " 'Odd' isn't the word I'd use. You . . . I'm so glad to see you. You look so wonderful—"

The intercom sounded, and Dan grimaced and answered the phone.

Marina stood up; she knew that for the moment she'd be more comfortable less close to Dan, for the closeness somehow added to her new perception of him as a handsome, apparently equally appreciative man.

As Dan spoke, she walked to the window once again, more comfortable with the view than with looking at him—at his handsome features smiling and then grinning, his athletic grace as he hopped off the desk and ran around to the other side to write something down, the sparkle in his eye she remembered from college. He was familiar and new all at once, someone she only half-knew, someone she felt vaguely uncomfortable with all of a sudden. The impersonal skyscape of the city was much easier, less challenging to look at, and she would concentrate on that for the moment.

But when she heard Dan replace the receiver and

she turned, his gaze met hers with an impact she couldn't ignore; the sensation felt somehow wrong, as if they shouldn't be looking at each other in that way; and at the same time it felt deliciously right. For his warm brown eyes at that moment were saying more than they had in all the time she had known him—warmly, deeply, with a fire that said, I want you.

"Come here," he said quietly, his eyes not leaving hers.

Her lips parted. "I . . ."

He came forward silently. When he reached her and put one arm gently around the small of her back, his eyes mirrored the wonder and desire in her own. Gently he put his other arm around her, with the same hesitancy, the same questioning, in his eyes. But when he lowered his mouth to hers, the warmth of his lips touching hers, there were no more questions, no more hesitations. The kiss was gentle, the lightest touch of lips to lips; but fire was beneath the lightness, and as Marina wrapped her arms around his neck and pulled him close, she let out a small cry of pleasure from somewhere deep inside. Dan drew his head back and for a moment looked at Marina in surprise and awe, his eyes heavy with desire. And then his eyes closed and once again his lips were on hers, then gently parting them as his tongue entered the warmth of her mouth and met hers in a thrilling touch that made them both moan.

Marina didn't question the kiss, didn't question what was happening. It felt more right, more wonderful, more exciting even in its lightest touch than any kiss she had ever had.

As the kiss deepened there was a growing heat between them, an urgency that drew them closer, quickened their breathing.

Dan tore his mouth away then and looked into Marina's eyes from under heavy lids. He inhaled deeply and smiled, but the smile was uncertain. "My God. I hadn't known . . . we would be like that. I just wanted to kiss you then. But . . ." He smiled and shook his head.

She gazed at him, her vision hazy from the pleasure of the kiss, feeling warm with desire.

"Had I known . . ." he said, grinning.

She smiled, but then her smile faded. She felt odd all of a sudden, having kissed the man who had been married to her friend, and with a hunger that suggested years of wanting and desire. She felt guilty, as if all those times she had been with Dan and Ellie, she had secretly wanted Dan, secretly wished he were hers; but it wasn't true.

"Dan," she said softly. "I—" She hesitated. What could she say? She didn't even know quite how she felt herself. But she knew it felt wrong, somehow.

He tilted his head and looked at her questioningly. "What's the matter?" he asked.

She shook her head. "I don't know. I feel odd, that's all. After all this time. . . ." Her voice trailed off.

"Look," he said, resting his hands gently around her waist. "Don't you think this feels a little odd to

26

me? Friends for a million years and suddenly the kiss of the century?"

She laughed.

"I'd like to see you, Marina," he said softly, his gaze holding hers, melting into her. "Not to push anything, not to force anything; just to see."

"I . . . don't know."

"You have to go up to Windy Hill. I'll come along. That's all. As a friend." He smiled. "Who happens to share something incredible with you, but a friend."

She laughed. "All right," she agreed. But silently she wondered. How could something feel so wrong and so right at the same time?

CHAPTER TWO

By the time the day to go to Windy Hill arrived,
Marina was exhausted from work and thoroughly
looking forward to a break. Her boss, Jean-Pierre
Massu, had brought his two young nephews from
France to learn the rudiments of the restaurant business over the summer, and the results so far had been
utter chaos. Massu's nephews—oafish boys of sixteen
and eighteen—moved through the kitchen like line-
backers, knocking pans, plates, and silverware to the
floor each time they turned around. And Massu had
been uncharacteristically quiet about the daily disas-
ters, maintaining a tight-lipped silence that infuriat-
ed Marina and the other employees. But she could
put it all behind her now—at least for a day—while
she visited Windy Hill with Dan. And she would put
aside the questions she had silently asked herself
after kissing Dan. Without these concerns she was

left only with a feeling of pleased anticipation—at seeing Windy Hill after all these years, and at being alone with Dan for the first time in years as well.

Just as Marina got a chance to glance at herself in the mirror and decide she wanted to change her outfit—she was wearing faded but well-fitted jeans, a boat-neck blue-and-white striped T-shirt, and sneakers—the doorbell rang. She looked at herself one last time—she really did look fine, with her slim figure flattered by the clothes she had worn so many times. But that was, unfortunately, just the point: she had worn the same sort of outfit in college—jeans and T-shirts, jeans and sweat shirts, jeans and flannel shirts—and she suddenly wished she had dressed a bit differently for this occasion that was, after all, eight years past her last day in college. But it was too late, and she knew that the clothes weren't, in any case, what was really bothering her.

No, what was bothering her was not her clothes, or her hair, or her lack of makeup; it was the memory of the kiss she had shared with Dan, of warm lips, warm breath, eyes filled with desire.

She took a deep breath and opened the door.

Dan smiled and stepped in, quickly taking her in from head to toe and then stepping past her into the foyer.

He looked wonderful—better, even, than he had the other day. He was wearing a light blue T-shirt and jeans, both close fitting but not too tight, showing off the firm outlines of his body without drawing too much attention.

They looked at one another, standing far enough

so they couldn't touch yet close enough to be palpably aware of the possibilities. His brown eyes sparkled, and then he smiled, a slow smile that grew as he came close, and she waited, breathless, as he stepped forward and then put his hands at her waist.

"You know," he murmured, half-smiling, "this is awfully silly." He leaned closer, his lips almost brushing hers.

She was achingly aware of the closeness of his body, his firm thighs radiating heat against her own, the strength of his hands, the warm darkness of his eyes. "What's silly?" she whispered, luxuriating in the heat that was enveloping her as his hands slid firmly along her back, pulling her closer, insisting that every inch of their bodies touch. Her breath came quicker as she looked into his eyes, gazed at his face, which was now serious—wondering yet knowing, questioning yet commanding.

"I think," he whispered, his breath light and warm against her lips, "I think we were meant for this a long, long time ago." He leaned down and gently kissed her neck, then rested his cheek against hers, roughness against silk. She pulled him closer, wrapping her arms around his neck, wanting to feel the heat of him everywhere. "And that's why it's silly," he whispered, "to pretend"—he softly touched his lips to hers and then drew back—"to pretend it's not true."

For a moment her gaze fused with his—simmering, melting, burning—and then, with a catch of her breath, she came forward and her lips met his in a blaze of heat. They both moaned with pleasure as they deepened the kiss, lips parting and tongues exploring in a dance of wanting. Her fingers plundered the softness of his hair as his hands roved along her back, over her hips, and then found the heat of her skin under her shirt. The touch was incredibly exciting, igniting her senses and dissolving her protests.

He pulled his mouth from hers and then pressed his lips against the smooth skin of her neck, the softness of her shoulder. "Marina," he whispered. "For so long." He raised his head and looked at her, his deep brown eyes darkening with concern. "You know, I don't even know if you're seeing anyone these days." He grinned. "Here I am doing my very best to make up for lost time, and that might be more than a small problem for you." His eyes shone. "You might not even want that," he added softly.

She smiled lazily; it was difficult to imagine wanting anything or anyone other than Dan at the moment. But then she remembered Barclay. "Well," she hedged, "actually, I—" She paused, and he smiled.

"Actually," he mimicked, raising a brow, "maybe I've made one too many presumptions. Maybe you don't even want to talk about it."

She shook her head. "No, no, that's okay. I guess I *am* involved with someone else."

He loosened his hold on her a bit, then strengthened it. "How involved?" he asked quietly.

She sighed. "I . . . I don't know. I met him only a few weeks ago, but"—she shrugged—"we've seen each other a few times, and we're going out tonight, as a matter of fact."

31

His eyes were somber. "Do you like him?" he asked.

"I . . . yes."

"Then do you really think you should be in my arms like this?" he asked quietly, his eyes daring her, his hands sending warmth through her veins.

She looked into his eyes, and slow smiles spread over both their faces. "Maybe," she said, laughing.

He kissed her gently on the lips, gave her a hug, and said, "Let's not make any issues out of anything. It's so nice to be together after all this time that it would be crazy to start questioning it."

She smiled. "I agree."

"Just one thing, though," Dan said, looking at her with challenge in his eyes.

"What's that?"

"At some point today you're going to tell me everything you know about this fellow."

She tilted her head. "Why?"

He smiled. "So I know what the competition is and how I can beat it."

Marina laughed. "I'm flattered, but you make it sound like a soccer game."

"Well, it's much more important"—he winked—"no matter how obsessed I was with the sport in college. But seriously, it's been a long time, and I don't even know what type of man interests you anymore." He smiled. "As I recall, neither of us understood the other's tastes back then."

"Well, who could have understood yours?" she asked, smiling. "Not including Ellie, obviously. But the rest—especially in freshman year! They were all beautiful, but some could barely tell time."

Dan shook his head. "I remember. But at one time or another I think I thought I loved each one of them." He gazed into her eyes. "Which shows just how wrong one can be, doesn't it."

Marina frowned. "But you didn't really think you were in love, Dan. When we used to talk about them, it was always a matter of a kind of deep liking and lust, as I remember." She smiled. "Or maybe lust and deep liking, in that order."

He smiled. "Or maybe talking with you brought me back down to earth," he said quietly. "There was always you, I think, to keep me from being serious with the others."

"Not with Ellie," she answered softly, half-questioningly.

He frowned. "No, not with Ellie," he murmured. He sighed, looking into her eyes.

They gazed at each other silently, each remembering hundreds of other times they had done the same. Marina wondered whether the attraction had always been so strong—though ignored and pushed aside—and whether the touching of feelings, sensations, thoughts had always been as it was now.

"I think that if we're going to go, we should go," he said suddenly. His eyes penetrated hers. "Or else we should stay here and spend the day."

Marina smiled—a bit nervously, she realized. "Uh-uh. That would be too easy. Don't you remember? Nobody—including the two of us—could figure us out back in college." She looked at him wryly. "As it stands now, it's been too easy already."

He smiled, but his eyes remained serious. "I honestly don't know how kissing you could be anything *but* easy, Marina. Or how—" He paused. "Well, those years are gone now."

The look was too deep, too mesmerizing, the gold-flecked brown of his eyes too hypnotic. Marina looked away. "Well. I just have a few things to get ready and then we can be off."

She gathered together her things—a beach bag with bathing suit and towel, in case it was hot, and a picnic that had been chilling in the refrigerator—and they were gone a few minutes later, heading north along the Hudson River in Dan's red Saab.

The drive up was easy and relaxed; the May air was pleasantly warm and deliciously fragrant on the back roads that Dan was taking, and for both Dan and Marina, worries about their jobs in the city gradually faded.

Dan glanced at her as the car rounded a curve. "You'd better brace yourself, you know."

"Why?" she asked.

He shook his head. "Because Windy Hill is probably not going to look remotely as you remember it. How long has it been since you were last there?"

"Oh, God. Let's see. It must be twelve years, because I was a freshman. My parents and I went up for a visit during that last summer. And then Tatiana said she was going to sell it, and she had a buyer, and that seemed to be it. She always led everyone to believe she had sold it, and to a very wealthy, reclusive man who wouldn't let any of us see what he had done with the property." Marina paused and looked at Dan. "I wonder why she went to such lengths to keep Windy Hill a secret. Do you know?"

He half-smiled. "In a way, though Tatiana liked to keep a lot of things to herself, so I was never sure whether she was pretending to 'fess up, as she used to put it, or not. But I know she had genuinely planned to sell Windy Hill, as she said in the will, until your parents had the accident. Then she didn't want to sell because she had an idea that somehow Windy Hill could bring the family—what was left of it—together. Then, when you and Alex started getting along worse than ever, she decided to throw the two of you together for a resolution."

"But why the secret, Dan? Why did she pretend to sell Windy Hill?"

Dan glanced at Marina for a moment; his eyes were evasive. Then he sighed. "I don't . . . I don't really know if I should tell you."

"What?" Marina said. "Are you kidding?"

"No, I'm not kidding," he said. "It was in confidence that Tatiana told me her feelings and wishes, Marina. Don't forget I was her lawyer."

"How could I?" Marina asked sharply. "And don't forget I'm her granddaughter—her only grand-daughter—and I have a right to know what she felt."

Dan sighed again. "Let's leave it for now," he said quietly. "You have to understand," he said overly patiently, "that what's spoken between lawyer and client is confidential—it's called privileged information—and—"

35

"Dan," Marina interrupted.

He looked at her. "What?"

"I may be a mere chef, but I *have* heard of attorney-client privilege. It's hardly an esoteric concept."

He sighed. "I'm sorry. I'm so used to explaining the most basic things. But there's no need to get offended." He shrugged. "If you explained some gourmet cooking terminology or whatever, it would be the same thing—except that I probably know a lot less about cooking than the average person knows about law." He smiled his most winning smile, something she had never been able to respond to with anything other than a smile or a laugh herself.

She sighed. He was right; she was oversensitive about being talked down to because it was something her ex-husband, Rick, had done almost constantly; but Dan was no more guilty of it than anyone used to explaining things in his work. "Sorry," she said, reaching over and touching him on the shoulder. "I guess I'm just not used to our being in different areas and hearing you talk like such a . . . I don't know. You're so different."

He raised a brow. "I should hope I am, Marina. And I can't help it if I sometimes sound like an attorney; that's what I am."

"*I* know that," she said. "I didn't even say anything about that."

He shot her a skeptical look. "You don't have to. I've felt your disapproval ever since I decided to become a lawyer, Marina. As if it's something absolutely dreadful."

"Oh, come on," she said. "That's ridiculous."

"It may be an exaggeration, Marina, but face it—you hadn't expected that from me when we knew each other, and you weren't happy with it when I made the decision. Even now you aren't comfortable with it."

She sighed. "Well, okay—you're right. But that's because I can't understand what happened. I don't want to sound like a Pollyanna, but you used to be such a fighter for the underdog all the time, so concerned with really great causes and things. What made you change?"

"*I* did, Marina, because of the life I had chosen—marriage, maybe kids, lots of things go along with those." He glanced at her. "I couldn't support my family on money from mountain-climbing, you know." He nodded his head in the direction the car was heading. "Though mountains like those are so dangerous one *should* be paid to climb them."

Marina looked up as the car reached the crest of the road and the full range of the Shawangunk Mountains came into view. The sight was breathtaking: the steep, often vertical cliffs were made of jagged rock in some places, cascades of huge boulders in others, all nestled in a wild-looking range covered with dark, spring-fresh trees. "Oh, Dan. I had forgotten how beautiful it is up here." She shook her head. "You know, the last time I was here with my parents—years ago—I was so furious about being shackled to them instead of being off with some fantastically handsome—and imaginary, I might add —man that I purposely ignored the scenery. I just blotted the whole thing out."

He laughed. "I used to do the same thing with my parents." He sighed wistfully. "But these mountains are pretty hard to ignore. This is the best rock-climbing in the Northeast. Dangerous, but fantastic while you're up there." He grinned. "And more so afterward, when you're safe on the ground and can exaggerate the perils for your friends."

"Well," Marina said, smiling, "I'll go along the footpaths and you can rappel your way up or whatever it is that you do."

He shook his head. "Uh-uh, not me. I'll be right there behind you. I'd be crazy to take it up now after all these years—without some sort of retraining, at least." He glanced at her. "Besides, I'd much rather be with you."

She smiled, and a few minutes later Dan turned the car down the narrow road leading to Windy Hill.

CHAPTER THREE

Dan had known he should warn Marina that Windy Hill might be different from what she remembered; but even he wasn't prepared for the sight. As he carefully steered the car along the overgrown gravel driveway leading to the inn, he was silent, as was Marina, shocked by the look of years-long abandonment. The whole property, from the collapsing clapboard structure of the inn itself to the landscaping around it, looked as if it had been attacked by both nature and vandals.

"Oh my God," Marina murmured, getting out of the car. "It's a wreck!"

Dan got out of the car and looked at the inn with obvious disbelief. "Marina, I don't know what to say. I knew it was in something of a state of disrepair, but this is unbelievable."

"Did Tatiana know it was this bad?" she asked quietly.

He shrugged. "I don't really know. She had been here fairly recently—a year or two ago—but it's hard to say when most of this damage happened." Marina joined him as he started making his way through tall grass and weeds toward the inn. "Most of this just looks like year upon year of neglect, mostly from storms," he said.

Marina was silent. The old inn had been virtually destroyed. She had thought—irrationally, she realized—that she would find what had once been: a lovely inn with huge shade trees on a sprawling, sun-drenched knoll; a place filled with mostly happy memories, a symbol of her past and perhaps her future. But it was almost unrecognizable.

The building itself was a long, rambling clapboard house from the 1880s, once white with green shutters and now mostly buff with chips of old, colorless paint. Most of the upstairs windows—especially those in the tiny gabled rooms on the third floor, where Marina had loved to play—were broken, and many of the shutters were dangling by one corner. The veranda—Marina's favorite part of the inn—had been stripped of all its old rocking chairs and now served merely as a very broken-down entrance to the old hotel. What had once been the lawn—remarkable because it was a huge, flat expanse of land at the edge of a steep mountain slope—was now wildly overgrown, with wildflowers and tall weeds swaying in the breeze.

Dan looked at her apologetically and then sighed.

"We might as well go in and get it over with," he said sadly. "I just wish it weren't such a disappointment. This must be very difficult for you."

"Oh, it's disappointing, but it isn't that bad," she said, as much to convince herself as him. "At least I have the inn—perhaps to keep—which is more than most people can say about a place they once loved a long time ago."

She followed him up the steps and onto the wide, once-gray veranda, and he turned. "You're not going to keep this place, Marina. But we'll talk about that later. Come on." He took a large, old-fashioned key out of his jeans pocket and unlocked the old wooden door, which opened easily and let out a mustiness Marina remembered well from the attic of the inn.

"How long have you had that key?" Marina asked, looking at Dan's handsome profile.

He turned and looked at her with mischief in his eyes. "Long enough so that I thought several times over the years of using it as an excuse to get back in touch with you"—he raised a brow—"even to sneak up here with you." He winked. "But that wouldn't have been particularly professional of me, now would it have?"

She smiled. "It would have been nice," she said, and winked. "And you could have trusted me with the secret." For a moment she had been about to say that, and it was probably exactly what Tatiana would have wanted. But that was silly, imagining that the old woman had planned such a thing.

"Well, let's hope we haven't missed our chance to take some pleasure out of what Tatiana left you," he said, and he stepped forward and opened the door the rest of the way.

Marina came in after him, and her heart sank.

The old commons room—a large, once-cozy room with a huge stone fireplace, a room that had once served as lobby, reading room, and main lounge—looked as if it had been destroyed. Beer bottles, empty rusted cans, broken glass, and even old pieces of charcoal lay everywhere across the floor. Surprisingly, the old Oriental rug was still there, shoved into a far corner of the room, but Marina could see it was threadbare and totally worn, held together only by a few miraculously strong fibers. Most of the windows were broken, and from fallen birds' nests and droppings Marina could see that the inn had been used by many creatures other than human beings. "At least the birds got some use out of the place," she said quietly, her voice barely audible. "That makes me feel a little better."

Dan put his arm around her and gave her a hug. "Come on. We'll survey the rest of the damage together."

With Dan's arm around her waist, Marina and Dan walked through the commons room into what had once been the library. Each pane of the bay windows had been broken; the window seats had been ripped out, perhaps chopped up for firewood, perhaps sold; and all the books were gone. "This was the library," Marina said quietly when she realized there were no clues as to what the room had once been.

Dan shook his head and led her on.

42

The dining room was in the same shape—empty, torn apart, the wallpaper ripped in jagged streaks from the walls.

"We're coming to the kitchen," Marina said as they walked through a small hallway. She stopped short in the doorway. "I don't believe it," she said. "The old stove is still here. And the sink!" She smiled and shook her head. "I guess it isn't so amazing," she said, "considering that they each weigh about a ton and a half."

She broke away from Dan to look at the old appliances, both of which were filthy but, she judged, probably still fine underneath.

When she turned to Dan, he was smiling, looking at her with an expression she couldn't read. "You know," he said, "seeing you light up like that almost makes me think you *should* keep this place. You look so happy."

She smiled. "Well, it's just that it all looked so terrible—absolutely everything I remembered was either gone or ruined—and I was happy to see something still here." She sighed. "But it's a pretty pathetic thing to be happy about, I guess," she said. "I had no idea it would be this bad, Dan. When you first told me and Alex about the inn, I had visions of running something that looked exactly as it had back then— you know, just driving up and opening the place up." She smiled sadly. "I wasn't thinking."

He looked into her eyes with affection. "Come on," he said. "Maybe it won't be so bad upstairs. And even if it is, Marina, we'll just go through it and then go outside and have that picnic you kept raving about on the way up. Then we can talk about what you're going to do with this place."

The second floor, however, was no better than the first. The few pieces of furniture that were left—a couple of dressers, some mattresses, a few tables—were so badly broken that even the people who had passed through had obviously felt they were unsalable.

After she and Dan had looked into each of the rooms from the hallway, Marina sighed and said, "Let's go outside and skip the rest. This is just too . . ." Her voice trailed off when her eyes met his. He looked much sadder than she felt; she was disappointed, but it wasn't the end of the world. Yet Dan looked as if he felt directly responsible, as if it were his fault the inn was in such poor shape.

He said nothing but merely followed her out to the car, where he took out the picnic things in silence. Then they walked out across the lawn through the wildflowers and the young trees to the edge of the woods, where they spread the blanket half under a huge old maple tree and half in the warm spring sun. "This is beautiful but not that practical," Marina said with a laugh as she and Dan tried to get the blanket to rest relatively flatly over the tall flowers.

Dan smiled. "Mm, but I don't think I much care about the blanket. Look at that—scarlet paintbrushes, larkspur, violets, primrose, pale meadow beauty"—he smiled and winked at Marina—"almost as beautiful as the dark meadow beauty standing next to me. And jewelweed over there, in case we get poison ivy."

"How do you know the names of all these flowers?" Marina asked.

Dan raised a brow. "If you spend any amount of time in the woods or hiking, you just pick it up here and there. And it's nice to know what's edible, what's an old Native American cure for whatever ails you—that sort of thing."

They eventually spread the blanket out with the help of all the dishes and baskets Marina had brought, and they sat down next to each other in the sun.

"Well," Dan said, smiling, "I hope this is better than the last picnic we had."

She raised her brows, pretending innocence, and asked, "Just which picnic was that?"

"You know very well which picnic," he said, narrowing his dark eyes and smiling. "Does burned chicken, sour potato salad, and warm beer ring a bell?"

Marina laughed. "The illustrious commencement of my career in fine cuisine. Mm . . . a meal to remember." She looked at him curiously. "But what really was memorable, Dan, was your reaction."

He smiled. "Which was—?"

"You ate and drank everything, pretending it was great until we both burst out laughing, as I recall."

He laughed and shook his head. "It really was awful. But I figured, well, she tried, and it was impossible cooking in those dorm kitchens. But the important thing, anyway, was being together, wasn't it?"

She looked into his eyes, hesitating, marveling, for the experience was so reminiscent of earlier times, yet so different, too. His eyes were the same but older, filled with something that had never been there before—wisdom, perhaps—that she found intriguing.

"Just as today," he continued, "was really an excuse—don't you think?—for getting together after such a long time apart." He sighed. "I just wish that Windy Hill were in better shape." His eyes darkened. "But let's enjoy the picnic and not think about the inn until later. You have a big decision to make, and you shouldn't rush it."

"I know," she said. She smiled and looked into his eyes. "So any distracting you do will be much appreciated."

He raised a dark brow. "Sounds good to me. And how, dear Marina, are you going to distract me?"

"Hm. Let's see. Well, how about a slightly better meal than our last picnic? I made broiled chicken with tarragon, rosemary, and sage; tomato and spinach tarts with thyme; celery rémoulade; and something very *un–cuisine minceur*—tollhouse cookies."

"That sounds fantastic," he said. "How can you look as great as you did in college if you make all those incredibly fattening-sounding things?"

She laughed. "Listen, it's not easy. If I didn't constantly watch myself I'd be a complete blimp. But actually, the main thing about *cuisine minceur* that's different from traditional French cooking is that it isn't nearly as fattening. You use herbs and stocks instead of heavy cream sauces and make everything really fresh and pretty with lots of fruits and vegetables; things like that make a huge difference." There was a spark of amused tolerance in Dan's eyes as Marina spoke, and she didn't know why. "What's the matter?" she asked.

He pursed his lips to suppress a smile. "Nothing. Except that I can see you're ready to wax poetic about the wonders of *cuisine minceur,* and I'm starved." He sat up and unwrapped the aluminum foil from the cold chicken and began opening the rest of the dishes. "My God," he said. "The smell alone is nearly enough to satisfy me. What did you put on all of this?"

"Oh, tarragon and thyme and rosemary and sage, with lemon and butter in the chicken—mostly lots of herbs, though. I grew them on my windowsill back in the city."

He looked impressed. Then he tasted the chicken, and Marina watched, pleased, as he closed his eyes and ate with an unmistakable look of sheer pleasure. When he looked at Marina, he shook his head and smiled. "I'm in a state of complete bliss. Marry me today and I'll be happy forever, Marina." She laughed. "You're a genius. Really."

Smiling, she helped herself to what she knew were shockingly large portions of everything. But she suddenly felt half-starved, and Dan's enthusiasm had only increased her hunger.

When she began tasting the food, each dish seemed better than the last. "Well, forget what I said about watching my weight. There may be a war for what's left of this food, Dan, because I'm suddenly starved."

"Uh-uh." He shook his head. "You have to keep

yourself svelte and beautiful for your date tonight with Mr. Right."

"I never said he was Mr. Right," Marina said, looking up at him. But she couldn't see his eyes; he was busy moving most of the containers to the side of him she couldn't reach. "Hey! Those aren't all for you!" she cried.

He glanced at her and shrugged. "I'm just saving you from yourself, Marina. If you really want this man to be interested in you, you're right to be careful."

"Are you saying I have to lose weight?" she asked.

He gazed into her eyes. "If it were up to me, I wouldn't change a thing." He paused, taking in her face, her hair, her breasts. "Not a thing," he said softly, musingly. "But then I've known you for years. I'm already crazy about you. You have to impress some bachelor-about-town who hardly knows you." He smiled mischievously. "Not that you'd have any trouble impressing anyone, Marina, but—"

"But what?" she interrupted mock-angrily. "I have this sinking feeling that you're putting yourself into Barclay's shoes—that you're visualizing my date tonight along the lines of the dates you have." She paused, remembering the night she had had to overhear Dan's conversation with another woman at that restaurant. "Maybe my dates are less interested in superficial qualities than you; maybe they don't have to know me for twelve years before they're crazy about me, as you put it." When she finished, she looked away for a moment, realizing she had perhaps gone too far. She had started out by pretending; but what she had said, she had meant.

Dan looked both confused and amazed. "What are you talking about? What superficial qualities? I was only kidding about looking good for your date." He winked. "Anything to keep you from the rest of this food," he said, helping himself to more salad. "What's bothering you, anyway? You knew I was kidding and you also know that I think you're damned pretty." He frowned, looking into her eyes. "So what's the problem?"

She took a sip of wine, trying to collect her thoughts.

"Hm?" he asked quietly. He reached his hand up to her glass and gently guided it down to the blanket. "Tell me," he said softly, his brown eyes tender.

"Oh, it's silly, really," she began, deciding to be honest. "Or not silly. But hard to say, I guess." She sighed. "It's just that I've never gotten used to how you changed after we stopped being friends. I don't mean in the way we've talked about—your becoming a lawyer and all that. I guess that . . ." She sighed. There was nothing she could say that wouldn't hurt Dan totally unnecessarily. She couldn't say that after college he had suddenly seemed shallow, overly ambitious, interested only in what the rest of upper-middle-class New York City seemed to be interested in. And sitting here with him now, it didn't even seem to be true.

"Marina, what?" he asked. "Tell me." His eyes glinted. "If I'm interested only in superficial things, clue me in on the details. If it's true, life will be a lot easier. I can go to singles bars and meet beautiful women I don't even like, engage in meaningless conversation until the right moment occurs, and then bring them into my charmed, superficial existence for an evening and one evening only. It'll be a lot easier than trying to meet someone I really care for, Marina."

She smiled. "All right, that's an exaggeration. But I know you do go to singles bars and things like that—I heard you mention some to that woman that night in the restaurant."

Dan raised an accusatory brow. "Eavesdropping?"

Marina nodded. "I couldn't help it." She paused and looked at him. "The whole time, as a matter of fact."

Dan smiled. "Me too. When Vanessa was talking, I was really listening to you or your date."

Marina laughed. "Look. Forget what I said. I sound as if I'm accusing you or judging you. And I don't have the right to, and I don't mean to, either."

He looked confused. "You sound as if you don't even know me anymore, Marina. I'm not going to apologize for the way I live—I like it—but I think you misunderstand it because so much time has passed, and when we were friends life was very easy. We lay in the sun, went hiking, went to class, and that was it. We didn't have to do anything special to meet people; we were in college and there were thousands to choose from. But things are different now. New York City isn't an easy place to meet people, and if you're like me and don't want to be involved

50

with anyone at the office, it makes things a lot harder."

He reached out and gently passed the back of his hand along her cheek, and for a moment her eyes closed as she inhaled his scent, felt the warmth emanating from his touch. "Of course," he added softly, gazing into her eyes, "if there were anyone like you at the office, I'd throw away my rules in a minute." She smiled, but his expression changed and he withdrew his hand. "Tell me about this Barclay." He paused. "Just how serious is it?"

Marina hesitated. "I told you it's only been a few weeks," she said. "It's hard to tell."

"Well, who is he? Where did you meet him? What does he do?" he asked with an edge of testiness she found flattering.

Marina smiled. "Jealous?" she asked.

"No." He frowned. "Well, yes." He sighed angrily. "I see you for the first time in ages and you've just taken up with some stranger."

Marina laughed. "He's not a stranger. He's a writer—poetry, short stories, mostly small-magazine things. But he's working on a screenplay right now. Oh, and he writes book reviews, too, mostly for papers out West, which is where he's been for the last several years."

She couldn't read Dan's expression. "How did you meet him?" he asked quietly.

"At a party—out in Sag Harbor when I was there for the weekend. But he's living in the city right now, so we've been seeing each other there." She reached out and picked a tall purple larkspur and began pulling off its petals. She shrugged. "But it isn't really something I would call serious," she said, looking at the flower rather than at Dan. One half of her felt as if she were lying, the other half as if she were being more truthful than she wanted to be. She liked Barclay enormously; yet something told her not to emphasize this fact to Dan, for her feelings for him ran deep after so many years of friendship. And she knew, too, that even if she were just thinking about Barclay rather than talking about him, she would still be cautious about her feelings. For she didn't trust her feelings about men anymore—not after so many wrong guesses, false starts, short periods of optimism that had ended in frustration and disappointment.

"Are you . . . seeing other people, then, or just Barclay?" he asked.

She glanced at him. "Well, no, just Barclay, but that's because there hasn't been anyone else I've wanted to go out with." She paused. "What about you?" she asked, smoothing out the blanket and lying down. "Are you seeing anyone special?"

He quickly shook his head. "Nope. And I never thought I'd say this, but I'm glad."

She frowned. "Why?"

He sighed and lay down next to her. "Because I'd rather give up the good things that come with a deep relationship and marriage than endure the bad, I suppose. I know that sounds awful, but it's true." He looked at her with regret in his eyes. "I never want to go through that again. Anyway, these days marriage means divorce as often as not. It just isn't that promising."

Marina looked at him in disbelief. "It's true about divorce, Dan, but you can't really mean what you said about giving up the good so you don't have to have the bad." She wondered silently whether he could possibly be voicing his true feelings. The Dan she had known and been so fond of would never have said something like that; but he had changed, and she had to remember that.

"I'm sorry to hear myself say it," he said quietly. "I certainly never thought I would." He hesitated. "And I can imagine how shallow it sounds. But I've had it—and I think it's only fair to let women I'm seeing know it so they don't have any expectations."

Marina gave him a withering look. "Not you, too," she said, and looked at him in mild challenge. "Do you think that's an original approach? Being 'honest' and 'out front' at the beginning, so there are no hurt feelings?"

He knit his brows. "I don't really know. I don't say it to be original, Marina. I say it so it's clear."

"Ah," she said. "And then everyone knows what the score is."

He looked at her directly, almost challengingly. "Yes, as a matter of fact."

"And what if you fall in love?"

He blinked. "You mean if *I* do, or *she* does?"

Marina widened her eyes in exasperation. "You do, she does, or—miracle of miracles—you both do. What then?"

He looked down at the ground, then into her eyes,

but evasively, as if he wished he were somewhere else. "I don't know," he said quietly. "I honestly don't know. It just hasn't happened. And maybe it never will." He paused. "I don't think Ellie and I were ever in love, Marina."

She stared. "Don't say that," she said quietly. "I'm sure it's not true." She turned away and pulled up another larkspur.

"Ellie has said it, too," he said softly. "It's not just me, Marina. And the marriage was something neither of us would care to repeat with anyone else."

Marina sighed and looked up at the inn, the decrepit old building on the brink of falling down; the fields around her, while more beautiful than ever with their heathery lavenders and oranges, were only a vague reminder of what had once been; and Dan, once someone with whom she had shared her most private thoughts, was expressing feelings and thoughts she would never have believed possible in him. It seemed all of a sudden as if everything and everyone had changed so much; she knew she, too, had changed, but in ways that didn't seem to fit the rest of the world.

They lay there on the blanket among the wildflowers, in a silence broken only by the calls of the birds and the soft rustling of the leaves in the gentle breeze, each thinking of what the other had said.

Finally Dan looked at Marina, her head bowed, dark lashes covering eyes he knew were as blue as the sky. "Marina . . ." he said, reaching out and covering her hand.

She turned on her side to look at him and said,

54

"Sorry. I was just thinking about how different everything is . . . How different we both are." She smiled sadly. "I'm not certain that I like it."

He rolled on his side to face her and stroked her hand, his own hand warm and wonderful and strong. "I know I don't like what I see in your eyes," he said quietly, "and what I hear in your voice." He reached up and caressed her hair, then ran his hand along her cheek, her neck, looking into her eyes with powerful warmth. "I know that I haven't stopped thinking about you since that day in the office . . . since that kiss." He frowned. "But I've told myself over and over again that nothing could ever work between us—not after we were such good friends."

He sighed. "I know that you didn't like what I said about relationships and Ellie and all that"—he paused—"but it's true. And because it's true," he said, his voice whisper-soft, his eyes melting into hers, "I keep telling myself I have to stay away from you." He moved his hand, tracing his fingers along her neck, up to her lips. His touch was warm, soft, exciting, and her lips parted. Desire spread through her, heating her limbs, enveloping her in breathless, hazy need, making her eyes heavy with wanting as she looked into his. "I've thought of your lips on mine and I can think of nothing else," he said softly. "Of the sweetness of your mouth, the heat of your body against mine." He inhaled deeply. "And part of me says stay away, and part of me says—"

"Don't," she whispered, reaching out for him. "Don't stay away."

"Marina," he whispered. And with a sigh of need

55

he moved forward and pulled her close. For a tantalizing moment his eyes bore into hers, their deep, clear gaze only increasing her wanting, telling her that the coaxing body she felt against her was ready to please her in every way she had ever dreamed, every way she had ever wanted. And then his lips covered hers, and the hard strength of his body insisted against hers with a need that was thrilling.

His tongue was deeply arousing in its urgent exploration of her mouth, and when it met with hers, the impact stirred her to warm, surging need. His teeth gently grazed her lips, feeding her desire with every touch, and then he sank his mouth wetly against her neck. "Oh Dan," she murmured hoarsely, "please."

"Tell me," he grated. "Tell me."

With an urgency that made her breathless, he moved on top of her. The strength of his hard thighs filled her with heated wanting, and she molded her body to his in desperate need to feel every part of his desire, every inch of his need. "I want you," she whispered into his ear, finding the warm flesh of his back with her questing fingers and moving lower. "I want you so much," she whispered, as her hands urged lower.

He raised his head and looked into her eyes with dark, stormy desire. "After all this time," he said huskily, his voice low and ardent in its caressing tone. "You're so beautiful—your eyes as filled with desire as mine must be, your heart racing."

"Dan," she whispered, and covered his lips with hers, wanting to feel that joining of need, melting of desires that was better than words, more exciting than his caressing voice. For his kiss was like fire, his lips warm and coaxing, his tongue sending waves of aching desire through her.

Silently except for moans of passion, sighs of desire, sharp intakes of breath, they worked heated magic upon each other. Fingers met flesh in searing touches, quested for responses that came quickly, violently; firm legs urged, parted, awakened with throbbing arousal; breaths came more quickly, shallow from their overwhelming hunger for each other, and Marina was suddenly engulfed in hot, shimmering, pulsating desire that had to be satisfied. "Dan," she urged. "I need you. I want you." Her voice came from deep inside, her words from a need greater than thought.

"Do you know you want me?" he rasped, his breath hot in her ear. "I have to be sure," he grated, biting her lobe and making her cry out. "I have to know," he murmured.

"I know," she whispered. "I know I've never felt this way—never wanted anyone so much—never needed anyone so much. I think I've always wanted you, Dan." He urged against her and sent a surge of liquefying fire through her. "I know I always have," she moaned.

"Oh God, Marina. There's nothing I want more than to please you . . . to please you and make you burn with pleasure the way I know you'd please me. But do you want me *now*, Marina—not in the past. Now—someone you don't know the way you used to—someone who's changed."

She opened her eyes and gazed at him, into the deep brown eyes filled with yearning, lips parted in hesitation, skin dark and damp from exertion. It was nearly impossible to concentrate with his strong desire so firmly evident, his breath so quick, both hearts beating so rapidly. She closed her eyes. What had he said? "Someone who's changed." He was warning her, telling her words she didn't want to hear, didn't want to think about. But as she realized he was right, that they didn't really know each other —not anymore—her desire began to ebb. For she couldn't make love with him—not so quickly, so soon after they had just met again. She wrapped her arms tightly around him and sighed, burying her face in his strong shoulder. "You're right," she said quietly. "We have to stop."

And slowly, reluctantly, they drew away from each other, unclasping arms, legs, desires as they looked into each other's eyes.

For the rest of the afternoon neither one mentioned the near-lovemaking; the heated looks and stirring touches as they explored the grounds and the inn once again were the only signs that it had ever taken place. The silence disturbed Marina, for it was a silence that, in a way, had existed for all the years of the relationship; would she and Dan wait another twelve years before acknowledging their attraction to one another?

But as Marina and Dan began exploring the lower fields of the lawn, just when Marina was about to say something, Dan took her arm and slid his hand into hers. "What next?" he asked, glancing at her with a spark of laughter in his eyes. "For two friends we've been remarkably uncommunicative over the years, and we're doing it now more than ever." He silently appraised her. "I'm not going to forget the way I felt a little while ago," he said. "Not ever. And I'm not going to let what we might have—what we could have in the future—just fall by the wayside."

She smiled. "What do you suggest?" she asked, looking up at him.

He hesitated, and she could almost see the spark disappear from his eye, the spirit leave him as he said, "We'll have to stay in touch about the inn if nothing else, so—"

She widened her eyes. "Dan, I'm not talking about the inn," she said, half-smiling over the ridiculousness of avoiding the subject of "them" once again. "And there's no need for cold feet. I'm the one with a date tonight, in case you've forgotten."

He laughed and pulled her to him. "All right," he said. "Caught in the act of evasion. So it's settled, then: we'll see each other soon, and talk about anything but the inn. How's that?" he asked, daring her with his eyes.

She smiled and shook her head. "If I didn't already know you and like you so much, I'd give up on you as a totally hopeless case."

CHAPTER FOUR

"Awkward" was the only word Marina could use to describe the rest of the afternoon with Dan. On the ride back they had laughed and joked and reminisced as easily as if they had been friends forever; yet each time one looked at the other in a certain way— remembering, rekindling the attraction, bringing forth their embrace as if they were embracing at that moment—the laughter would stop, the gaze would deepen, and suddenly they were as self-conscious as could be.

But Marina didn't care; it was exciting and challenging to be with Dan again, discovering aspects of him she had never known and reacting to him for the first time in her life as she always could have but never had—as a woman with an attractive, interesting, and interested man.

When he had dropped her off at her apartment, he

had joked about not going in because his feet were too cold, and she knew that there was truth in his humor. But she didn't care about that, either. For she didn't know the extent of her interest in him; she knew only that he was someone she wanted to see more of . . . and someone whose kiss, whose warm lips and urgent desire she would think of often.

Later, as she hurriedly showered for her date with Barclay, she realized with amazement that there were suddenly two men in her life, after what had seemed like ages and ages of none. Perhaps it wasn't just chance, she thought; perhaps she was involved with Barclay and Dan because she was finally ready, after the unpleasantness of the divorce from Rick, for a new relationship. Now what she had to be wary of, she knew, was coming on too strong. For lately she had felt almost possessed by the desire for a good, deep, and lasting relationship with a man—something she hadn't felt since she had married Rick, and something she had thought she'd never feel again. She would have to be certain, if she became deeply involved with Dan or Barclay, that it was the man she loved rather than the idea of a relationship; and she would have to be certain as well that she didn't scare anyone off by her enthusiasm. Over the years she had read such advice in column after column and magazine after magazine and resented it: why couldn't people be honest with each other and say what they really felt? But she had run scared herself many times over the years, ending relationships that might have gone somewhere simply because she was so wary and mistrustful. And she knew that men could be scared off as easily as she.

What amazed her, though, as she dressed, was that both Barclay and Dan seemed to be so good; she had gone out with so many less-than-honest men over the years—before, after, and including Rick—that it was almost uncanny that she was now seeing two essentially decent men—honest, kind, intelligent, good-looking, exciting. Amazing.

And Barclay, when he arrived, was, if not amazing, at least very pleasant to see. Blond, with beautiful pale blue eyes, he was tan and healthy-looking, affectionate and relaxed as he took Marina in his arms and kissed her lightly on the lips. He had brought flowers—daffodils from Sag Harbor—and had said as he handed them to her that he had thought of her all week long.

Now as they sat next to each other on Marina's couch, sipping white wine and eating cheese and crudités, Barclay was suddenly quiet and uncharacteristically withdrawn. When Marina talked, telling him about Tatiana and Windy Hill, he seemed hardly to be listening, and when it would have been natural for him to say something, there was merely silence.

"Is anything wrong?" Marina finally asked.

He didn't look at her. He took another sip of his wine and then stroked his chin, which was unshaven and rough-looking. He glanced at her for a moment, then looked down into his glass. "Marina, I really like you," he said, still not looking at her.

Her heart sank. He was speaking with such reluctance and regret that he could only be leading up to one point: that he wanted to stop seeing her. Damn.

"Barclay, is this some sort of good-bye?" she asked quietly. She wished she could see his eyes.

He shook his head. "Not at all," he said. "At least I hope not."

"I don't understand."

He sighed and refilled his glass. "Look, I can't tell you how sorry I am about all this—but before we get in any deeper, it's important that you know." He shook his head. "I wish things weren't so good between us—that I didn't like you so much." He sighed. "And that I had been more honest." He looked up and turned his blue eyes upon her. "I'm married, Marina."

She blinked. "What?" For a moment she thought he was telling her he had just gotten married, that some fluke had turned everything upside down. But then she realized that he meant he was and had always been, in the time she had known him, married.

"Marina." He picked up her hand and held it in both of his. She extricated herself and faced him as he said, "I didn't tell you about it before because I just didn't know how involved we'd be."

She stared at him. "And what then? If we got involved, you'd tell me, but if not I'd be none the wiser and it wouldn't matter?" She shook her head. "That sounds just great, Barclay."

He sighed. "It sounds worse than it was. I didn't . . . well, it wasn't planned like that. If I had planned it like that, I suppose it would have been awful." He paused and took another sip of his wine. "It was just that I didn't want to tell you . . . I kept putting it off, and now here we are."

"Mm. Here we are," she said. "I can see how it happened; it isn't as if we saw each other a hundred times before you said anything. But just because I understand how it happened doesn't mean—" She sighed. "All I know is that I'm angry." She looked into his eyes and fought against his deep blue look of desire, a look that made her angrier than anything he had said. For he was a manipulator, a man who knew he could go far on his looks. "I'd like you to leave," she said.

He gazed at her steadily. "Are you sure?" He reached out and gently caressed her cheek.

She reached up and took his hand away. "Believe me, I'm positive," she said. "And I think I deserved to be asked that question a long time ago." She frowned. "Where is your wife, anyway?"

"She's still in California."

"Then you're separated—?"

He shrugged. "To be honest, no. Not really. She had some business out there and we decided I'd make the move East without her. But no, we're not separated." He hesitated. "Would that have made a difference?"

She glared at him. "I don't run my life by some book of rules, Barclay, where single's fine, married is out, separated is borderline. What makes a difference now is that you *are* married, and that's that. I'm not interested."

He poured more wine for both of them. "Can I tell you a story?" he asked quietly.

She hesitated. "I—" she began. "I really . . . oh, never mind. Just tell the story and then please leave."

"All right." He took a sip and then leaned forward. "I've been married a long time, Marina. My wife and I have both had affairs, and we're pretty open about it—we don't flaunt anything in front of the other person, but we don't have too many secrets, either." He paused. "Most people—most women—feel that an affair always ends in hurt feelings and unhappiness, but—"

"Wait a minute," she interrupted. "I don't think I want or need to hear this. Is the moral of this story going to be that we can have an affair and it might turn out to be beyond my wildest dreams of happiness and fulfillment?"

He sighed. "When you put it like that, Marina—"

"It sounds as ridiculous as it is," she finished. "Just forget it. I don't know why the idea that I'd like to have a relationship with an unattached man is so outrageous or hard to understand."

He gazed at her levelly. "It isn't hard to understand, Marina. But sometimes people have to break the rules when something's really worthwhile."

She sighed and stood up. "I'm sorry, Barclay, but at this point I don't think it would have been. And I'd appreciate it if you'd leave."

He tilted his head. "I'll call you again," he said with a question in his voice. He stood up and approached her as if to kiss her.

"What's the point?" she said, turning away and

walking toward the door. "I don't mean to be harsh, Barclay, but under the circumstances . . ."

He picked up his wine and drained the glass, then picked up his jacket. "I'm sorry, Marina."

"Good-bye," she said. "I'm sorry, too." She watched him leave and then shut the door.

Marina's anger was mixed with a healthy dose of relief—relief that she had found out he was married before she had become seriously involved with him, and even greater relief that she had found out he wasn't the wonderful man she had built him up as in her mind. Most of all she was annoyed with herself: while she had thought she was in a new phase of her life, open to promising relationships for the first time, she hadn't, in fact, changed a bit. She was still choosing men who were wrong for her in some way, setting herself up for sure disappointment, just as she had in her marriage and all the relationships she had had before and after.

She collected the glasses and bottle from the coffee table, noting with uncharacteristic and irrational pettiness how much wine Barclay had drunk, and brought them into the kitchen. Just as she started washing the dishes, the phone rang, and she wondered for a moment whether it might be Barclay. He had seemed remarkably unaware of her annoyance and disappointment, and it was thus altogether likely that, though she had asked him not to, he would call again, and this quickly.

But it was her boss, Jean-Pierre Massu, on the line. "Marine," he whined, never having said her name correctly. "Marine, we have not been able to call you all day long. Where have you been?"

"I was out," she said simply. "What's wrong?"

"Chaos, Marine, chaos, and you must come back tomorrow for the luncheon."

"The luncheon?"

"The lunch, Marine. My compatriots from France have come, and they stay only until tomorrow. I promised them the luncheon made by you. We are closing off the dining room in the back, Marine. I have made arrangements for you to go to the market at five tomorrow morning. You will meet Raoul in my car." He paused. "It would have been much preferable if you had been here for dinner tonight, Marine. I am sorry things have worked out so poorly. And in the future you will please be available by the telephone on your off days."

"Days off," she corrected. "But what does that mean—'available by telephone'?"

"That means this, Marine. If I call you, you will be able to come and prepare the dinner if I have customers as important as our friends tomorrow."

"But then it isn't a day off, Monsieur Massu. For instance, today I was up in the country. There would have been no way—"

"I am certain you will find a way, Marine," he cut in. "To keep one's position of great prestige, one always finds a way. Raoul will pick you up on your street tomorrow, and we will see each other some time afterward."

She sighed. "All right," she said reluctantly, knowing she had no choice. "But I'd appreciate it in the future if you'd give me more advance notice if I'm to prepare lunch and go to the market. It's really quite late for that, and—"

"There are many—how do you say?—bitter pills we must have in life. I, too, wish we had had more notice. If I had reached you today, you could have been leaving the restaurant by now. Good-bye, Marine."

She hung up and cursed. Now, in addition to everything else, she'd have to get up at four A.M. and drive out to the Hunts Point Market to select vegetables and fruits with the more obnoxious of Massu's two nephews. And though she had wanted to object more strenuously, she had known it would have led nowhere but perhaps down, for Jean-Pierre Massu required a good degree of passivity in all of his employees except the clumsy Raoul and Alfonse. The chef who had taught Marina most of what she knew had quit in disgust only weeks earlier and had warned Marina that if she took his place, she would have to be prepared to take a tremendous amount of unwarranted criticism. And that had been before Massu's nephews had come to make the situation even worse.

The phone rang again, and Marina cursed once more. It had not been her night so far. "Yes," she said angrily.

"Gee, I don't know, Marina," came Dan's voice. "That sounds like a very thinly disguised no to me. What's the matter?"

"Oh, nothing. Everything. Let's just say it hasn't been the most successful night of the year so far."

"What happened? I thought you'd be out—I was going to leave a message on your answering machine —not my favorite pastime, by the way. But what happened with Barclay?"

"Oh . . ." She hesitated and then said, "He's married, Dan. Which I suppose I should have known."

"Why?" he asked. "All the signs but you didn't see them, or what?"

"Actually, no," she said, carrying the telephone over to the couch and lying down. She was beginning to relax for the first time that evening. "I don't think there were any signs—no particularly evasive answers, no white stripe of skin where a wedding band usually is—nothing like that. And I think the reason he seemed so unmarried was because he basically thinks of himself that way."

"Then why should you have known?" Dan asked. "You're being too hard on yourself."

She sighed. "Because he was—or seemed—too good to be true," she said. "And I think it's almost true that all the good ones are married, as they say."

"Thanks a lot."

She smiled. "I said 'almost.' Anyway, in the end he turned out to be not that great anyway. Much less than not that great, even."

"Hm. Well. I don't want to sound smugly pleased, but I am. Tell me, did your discovery come before, during, or after dinner?"

"Before, unfortunately. Or fortunately, I guess."

"Very fortunately for me. Still hungry?"

She smiled. "Starved."

"Great. I'll pick you up in half an hour, all right?

I've been working late and I'm still downtown. Where do you want to go?"

"Anyplace but L'Aigle d'Or, where I work," she said.

"Okay, we'll test the culinary expert's taste buds on my favorite restaurant."

"Great. See you in a while."

She smiled. Maybe the evening wouldn't be so bad after all.

Dinner, at a tiny Italian restaurant Marina had never even heard of, was delicious and relaxing, exactly what she needed in order to forget about Barclay and Jean-Pierre Massu.

She and Dan had gnocchi in pesto, osso bucco, and arugula salad, and Marina agreed with Dan that it was the best Italian food she had ever had in New York.

After the espresso arrived, Dan took Marina's hand in his and looked into her eyes with affection. But there was a flash of humor in his eyes as well, and he just barely suppressed a smile as he said, "Is this our first real date, or do we count the time we almost kissed outside of Commons that night in college?"

She smiled. "Almost kissed? Thanks a lot!" She had, though, forgotten the entire incident.

Dan laughed. "Well, it *was* one of the more awkward moments of my life—beforehand, during the half-second it lasted, and afterward."

She laughed. "I guess we weren't ready."

His gaze was heavy with desire, dark with yearning as he said, "It seems hard to imagine. Although

70

I know it's true. Just as I know I was looking for a reason to call you tonight."

She smiled. "Why do you need a reason?"

He gave a short laugh. "Are you kidding? I needed a reason to tell myself. Old Cold-Feet Sommers can't call a woman the evening after he's spent the whole day with her." He winked. "That's much too soon; it breaks all the rules. Besides," he said and shrugged, "I thought your writer friend would be there."

"Mm." She made a skeptical face. "So what was the un-ulterior motive, then?"

"Well, I called Alex," he said, steepling his fingers on the table. "He had said he'd call me about the will—some specifics about the inn he wanted to know. Anyway, he hadn't called, so I thought I'd check in with him." He sighed. "I'm sorry I did."

She frowned. "Why?"

"Oh, for one thing, I think it stirred him up—the lawyer for the estate calling and all that. It makes the issue of Windy Hill seem more important than perhaps it actually is. But also the timing couldn't have been worse. He told me that a deal of his had fallen through not more than five minutes before, and it was more important than ever that Windy Hill be sold. And he asked me to do what I could to convince you to sell."

She raised a brow. "And? What did you say?"

"I told him I had done all the advising I was going to do. Which isn't true, but he doesn't have to know it. Your brother is not my favorite person in the world, Marina."

71

She sighed. "Well, he really . . . he just needs to grow up. He's very young—a very young twenty-seven, not at all in touch with the way he feels. Obsessed with money and with being a success, but I don't think he's really like that."

Dan shot her a quizzical look. "Well, he may not be, but he was very adamant over the phone."

Marina shrugged. "He's very adamantly against anything I'm for, very much in favor of anything I'm against."

Dan looked into her eyes questioningly, searchingly, and then he seemed to relax, as if he had come to a decision. "Marina, you don't have to decide about the inn for a while; certainly not tonight. So let's talk about it another time, all right?" he asked softly. "There's so much I want to get to know about you all over again, to ask you about; it seems silly to talk about business—and about something we might strongly disagree on. Let's just enjoy being together." He sipped his espresso and glanced into her cup, which was empty. "If you're in the mood, we can walk up Columbus Avenue from here and have a nightcap."

She smiled. "Sounds nice." But silently she wondered why Dan was so disturbed about the idea of her keeping Windy Hill; for she didn't want his feelings about it to interfere with the relationship.

When they left the restaurant and headed north, Marina looked up at Dan—strong-jawed, masculine, obviously possessing a great deal of inner and outer strength—and she wondered whether this strength

—his sense of responsibility for others—might in fact be a burden to him and to his relationships.

As he took her arm and smiled down at her, she spoke. "You know, I don't want to talk about Windy Hill now, either," she said, enjoying the easy feel of walking along with him, "but I just want to say one thing."

He smiled and raised a brow. "Uh-oh. Famous last words—'I just want to say one thing.' That's usually a sure signal for a thousand additional comments."

"Well, this isn't. It's just that you seem so concerned about what happens with me and Windy Hill —more so than if I were just someone you didn't know."

He frowned. "Well, obviously, Marina. I care very much about what happens to you and what you do. And what happens with Tatiana's estate as well. Does that really strike you as odd?"

She shook her head. "No, that isn't what I meant. I'm glad you care, Dan. But you sound as if you feel somehow responsible for whatever the outcome will be. And it isn't your responsibility. Whatever decision I make will be mine alone."

He looked at her and smiled, surprise and affection in his eyes. "I'll keep that in mind," he said.

She smiled. "Good. Because I mean it. If your fear is fear of being committed, mine is of being smothered. You didn't know Rick all that well, but he left nothing—*nothing*—up to me, and it really destroyed us. Because who, really, can bear all that responsibility? I couldn't stand to give it to him, he hated it, and he resented the hell out of me."

Dan shook his head and drew her closer against him. A moment later, when they stopped at the curb for a red light, he looked down at her and then leaned down and kissed her lightly on the mouth. The kiss was soft, delicious, filled with promises, and when she opened her eyes and looked into his, she wished she could fall into his arms and begin to make love as they had up in the country.

He smiled with wonder. "Now I remember why I always loved talking to you about all those ridiculous relationships I used to have," he said. "You've got one hell of a head on your shoulders—and it's as easy on the eyes as any I've ever seen." He took her arm again and held her close as the light changed and the nighttime crowd shifted forward.

From Lincoln Center they walked east and then headed up Columbus Avenue, once a wide boulevard dotted with modest neighborhood shops but now dominated almost completely by trendy, expensive stores that catered mostly to passers-through rather than neighborhood residents. Card and gift shops had replaced groceries; clothes and sports boutiques had displaced the local candy stores, and restaurants serving everything from Szechuan to Sudanese food had spilled over onto almost every square foot of sidewalk. Marina hadn't liked the avenue since the change had occurred, but she did enjoy it for the people-watching it provided: on any given night of the week hundreds of people—natives and tourists of all different backgrounds—came to sample the restaurants and then settle in at the sidewalk cafés or stroll slowly up and down the avenue doing what everyone else was doing: looking at each other and being looked at.

"There's a place along here that I really like," Dan said as they snaked their way through the crowds. "It has outdoor tables that are pretty hard to get, but they're worth waiting for just for the view."

When they arrived at the restaurant, with dozens of tiny umbrellaed tables taking up almost the entire pavement, Marina was surprised. As far as she knew, it was a singles bar, and judging from the clientele—extremely well-dressed women and men mostly in suits—that was what it was.

Dan managed to find them a table, and soon they were ensconced in a sea of people very conscious of observing and being observed. Marina noticed that Dan blended in without a trace—a handsome man in his late thirties, well-dressed and prosperous, definitely on the way up in the world. It bothered her, not fitting at all with her image of the "true," mountain-climbing Dan, but she tried to put it out of her mind. She had enjoyed everything about the evening so far, and it was silly and destructive to start setting store in superficial qualities that couldn't even really be called faults.

Yet she began to wonder as she looked around at the women at the surrounding tables: were they the sort Dan found attractive? And if so, did she have anything in common with them? From what she could glean from their looks and conversation, they were almost sharklike in their acquisitiveness and interest in the men there, playing something that looked to be a very serious game.

After the drinks came, Dan looked at Marina and asked, "Well, how do you like it?"

Marina smiled. In a certain way she was definitely —and unexpectedly—enjoying the place. When she looked at Dan and saw a familiar gleam of challenge in his eyes, she didn't hesitate to respond. "I'll bet you assume I can't stand this place."

He shrugged. "How could you? It's flashy, trendy, expensive—"

She laughed. "However," she interrupted, "I can't help it—it's nice being able to observe so openly, and to see New Yorkers at their worst and best walking by."

He sipped his drink and glanced around. "I don't see anyone I know tonight. Although we're here later than I usually am. Generally if I come here, it's after work."

She looked around for a few moments at the people at the other tables, then looked at Dan and winked. "Feel as if you blend in?" she asked, smiling. "On the surface—in terms of appearances alone— you do."

He smiled. "You're so sure everyone here is so terrible, Marina. Why?"

She shrugged. "I don't know. I guess I shouldn't make judgments so quickly. But I suppose more than anything else it's because I feel out of place, as if neither one of us fits in. Everyone else is sizing everyone up, making a decision, and boom, moving in or moving on to someone else. I can't see you doing that sort of thing."

He smiled. "I do it as well as anyone else, Marina,

76

which isn't very well at all. But it beats going home to an empty apartment." He sighed. "Anyway," he said, gazing into her eyes, "there's one thing we don't have in common with anyone here." He reached out and took her hand in his, then raised it and held it against his warm, rough cheek. She felt suddenly as if she were alone with him, as if his smooth, low voice and velvety brown eyes were for her and her alone, as if his touch—melting, warm, as with his other hand he caressed her knee—were meant to urge her into his arms, to press her lips against his. She wanted him then, wanted to feel the strength of his thighs, the urgency of his need, the tremors of desire she had felt with him before.

"Everyone here," he said softly, "is looking for someone. Searching . . . and searching some more." He inhaled deeply, his gaze heated, ardent. "In a sense, deep down, we've known for a long, long time, Marina, without realizing it. I want you," he said, his voice low and husky. "I want you and I'm sure of that."

She looked at him, caught in his gaze, achingly without protest under his heated touch, thinking only of the rapturous, breathless fervor they had shared.

He brought his hands to her cheeks and held her eyes with his. "I can see it in your eyes, Marina. I can hear it when your breath catches as I touch you."

"I can't think," she murmured. "I can't think straight with us here instead of . . . alone." She took a deep breath, trying to stop her heart from beating so quickly, trying to steady herself. "We could go

77

back to my apartment," she said quietly, her voice thick with desire.

His gaze was steady, warm, thrilling. "I think that sounds just about right," he murmured hoarsely.

They held hands as they left the restaurant and began walking up the avenue once again. But this time neither one paid any attention to the shops or the restaurants or the people. Each was caught in a fantasy they knew was theirs to fulfill, deeply, in heated abandonment, with whispered desires, pulsating rapture.

The moment they were inside Marina's apartment and Dan had shut the door, he took her in his arms as she had ached for him to do all evening; she took him into her arms with hunger.

"Marina," he murmured, his breath soft, his cheek rough against hers. "Every time I have you in my arms I wonder how I could ever let you go." He kissed her just below her ear and then moved his mouth downward as she wound her fingers in the softness of his hair. "More than anything else I want you to feel the same way."

"I do," she murmured. "You know I do."

"Oh God," he rasped and closed his lips over hers as she had thought of over and over again since he had kissed her that first time in his office, ached for through long nights when she could think of nothing else.

Their bodies were fired by the memory of their past embraces, and each grasped, stroked, urged with greater need, greater certainty, and responded with a hunger born of days and nights of deprivation.

He tore his mouth from hers and gazed into her eyes. "Come," he urged, and with a warm hand at the small of her back, he guided her to the couch. For a moment as she lay down and looked up at him, growing warm under his hungry gaze, she had a moment of hesitation—it was still too soon to make love, still too early to give herself, to melt with him as she so desperately wanted to. But as he planted his knees to either side of her, his firm thighs braced against her hips, she knew only that she had to have him, to feel the hard strength in front of her urging her to heights of passion and ecstasy that made her breathless.

His eyes were dark, ravenous as he looked down at her.

"Come," she whispered, reaching for him.

He inhaled deeply, his eyes roving over her eyes, her mouth, her breasts, and he murmured, "When it's time, Marina, when it's time."

She grasped his firm thighs with hands hungry for his touch, and his eyes closed as her fingers worked up and down his length. "Marina," he rasped, and he opened his eyes. Hungrily he unbuttoned her blouse, and when he parted it and exposed her naked breasts, desire surged through her. "You're so beautiful," he whispered. "So beautiful." His fingers gently traced the soft rise of each breast, catching each nipple and then tantalizingly brushing past, and then with a moan he descended, his lips taking over where his fingers had been. With each gentle bite, each flick of the tongue on her nipples, her ardor grew, and she raked her hands along his strong back with fierce need. His fingers found the flesh beneath her skirt and kneaded the tender, sensitive skin of her thighs with an urgency that sent hot liquid need through her, and she cried out in desire. She whispered his name into his hair, his ear, softly against his lips as he moved upward, fitting his body to hers with thrilling strength.

"All day," he murmured, "all day I've wanted this—to look at you, to touch you, to know from your eyes and your touch that you felt the same."

As he worked his hands up along her thigh, she was overtaken by a flowing, burning need that made her hoarse and breathless as she moaned, "I felt the same way."

"I wanted so much to make love with you up at that house—in that field—everywhere. Every place seemed perfect for love, perfect for taking you and giving you pleasure until you couldn't take any more."

She urged him on, aching to melt into his firm desire, desperately wanting her yearning joined with his. "I wanted you, too," she whispered. "I didn't want to leave."

"I shouldn't have let you," he murmured. "I should have told that Barclay to go to hell."

She loosened her hold on him then, opened her eyes as suddenly as if she had been slapped.

"What is it?" he asked, drawing his head back and gazing into her eyes. "What's the matter?"

She sighed, frustrated, sorry, hazy, as uncertainty began to take the place of flushed desire. She shook her head and gazed into his eyes. "When you mentioned Barclay, I—" She hesitated, suddenly unsure of how she felt.

He frowned. "Did you care about him more than I thought, Marina?"

She shook her head. "That isn't it." She sighed, realizing the import of her words. No, she didn't care much for Barclay now; his insensitivity had seen to that. But she *had* cared for him, and—optimistically, she now realized—she had fantasized things that would have come with loving him—making love, even marriage. For even though she hadn't loved him, and those thoughts had thus been premature, she had been aware of the promise of love, the potential for much, much more. And she had been wrong. As she always had been before, even in marriage. She had moved too quickly with Barclay, unconsciously assuming things that weren't true: and thus she had been destined for disappointment. And the realization stung all the more because she knew she was doing it with Dan now—the same evening, of all things—when she might have learned something instead.

"Marina," he murmured, "please tell me."

She turned her eyes up to his, her own filled with regret while his were clouded in confusion and concern. "I'm sorry," she said. "It's not . . . particularly good timing. Not specifically because I was out with Barclay tonight, but because I—I realize I'm moving too fast." She inhaled the scent of him—of desire mixed with exertion—and wished that what she was saying weren't true; but she couldn't deny it. "There are things"—she hesitated—"there are things that haven't been resolved between us—things I have to find out about." She sighed, trying to find the words.

He put his index finger gently over her lips. "It's all right," he said softly. "You don't have to explain yourself as if you're on trial."

She smiled. "You're right. And anyway, we've waited twelve years, so we can wait twelve more, right?" She winked and widened her eyes. "I'm only kidding," she said with a laugh, kissing him lightly on the mouth.

He pulled her close and held her gaze. "Just promise me one thing," he said, his voice hushed.

"What's that?"

"That eventually, when the time is right for you," he murmured huskily, "you decide we were meant to make love."

She sighed, saying nothing, wondering only when she would be sure enough of her feelings to let herself go.

CHAPTER FIVE

It was only when Dan had gone that Marina remembered she had to be up at four A.M. the next morning. Since it was already after midnight when she finally got into bed, she decided it was too late to worry about getting enough sleep: there was now no way that she could.

And she knew, too, that she was far too energized to sleep; her mind was filled with arguments, her body aroused by the physical memories of Dan's urgent caresses. And as the memories grew stronger, she wondered how she had been able to resist the deep fulfillment of lovemaking. Every coaxing stroke of his hands, every urgent movement of his body, each warm, deep kiss had been more exciting than the last—and all more arousing than any she had ever experienced.

But she couldn't act on physical desire alone; and

she'd have to remember she hadn't changed as much as she had thought: the experience with Barclay had shown her that she wasn't nearly as good at assessing men as she had thought, and she was still setting herself up for disappointment, choosing men who were ultimately wrong for her.

When she finally fell asleep she dreamed of Dan in many guises, all unidentifiable but all compelling, captivating, beguiling. In all the dreams he looked like Dan, but in some important respect he was someone else—a stranger, a foreigner, a lover. And in each he was magnificently pleasing, someone whom, when she awakened, she wanted to draw close and cover with long wet kisses.

But in each he had been a dream figure, she had to remember. And groggily, as she roused herself out of bed in the predawn darkness, she warned herself that Dan couldn't be as wonderful as he had seemed in her dreams. Most of real life, in fact, wasn't as beautiful as it had been in her dreams.

And the trip to Hunts Point Market with Raoul Massu did nothing to dispel that feeling. There was nothing wrong with the market itself, or even with the idea of the journey. Many, if not most, good chefs in the city went at dawn every day, not trusting the crucial selection of the finest, freshest fruits and vegetables to anyone but themselves. Marina had loved going to the market when she was the luncheon chef at L'Aigle d'Or. But then she had always gone with one of her assistants, all of whom she liked.

The presence of Raoul Massu, however, changed the entire tenor of the trip. From the moment he picked Marina up, Raoul—eighteen years old and weighing at least 225 pounds—acted as if Marina were merely accompanying him as some sort of servant rather than as a highly skilled chef, in charge. He had virtually ordered her to be back at the car by a certain time, and when Marina had said she wanted him to come along to wheel the large cart, he had looked at her in great surprise and said, "But I am the nephew of Jean-Pierre Massu."

"Well, I am the chef of L'Aigle d'Or," she had said carefully, "and if you don't help me, L'Aigle d'Or isn't going to have the very important luncheon that your very important uncle has promised."

That kept him quiet for a bit, but later on that morning, when Marina had been at the restaurant for a few hours, Monsieur Massu approached her in the kitchen. "Marine," he said quietly in his misleadingly soft voice, "Raoul has told me that the market was not altogether pleasant this morning."

She stopped stirring the herb dressing she was preparing for the cold asparagus spears and looked at Massu with the most innocent expression she could muster. "Oh, really?" she asked. "I thought it was rather nice this morning—nice weather, an excellent selection of vegetables—" She gestured at the asparagus. "Just look at these."

His face reddened. "Marine, that is not what I am talking about. Raoul says you were quite rude."

She put down her knife and looked Massu straight in the eye. "I know what you're referring to, Monsieur Massu. I thought you might realize what you were saying and decide to forget it. But if you want to discuss it, fine. Raoul didn't want to help cart the vegetables; I had naturally assumed that was why he was there, and I made it clear in the best way I knew how that I expected him to help. I don't see anything wrong in that, and I'm sure you don't either."

Massu's lips tightened. He reached down and picked up a spear of asparagus. Then he dipped it in the dressing, took a bite of it, and said nothing.

Marina almost smiled. This, apparently, was his greatest insult. But then he spoke.

"Marine, you are my chef and you have a right to expect the assistance. But you will not speak rudely to my nephews under any circumstances. This is not a question I wish to debate." He finished the asparagus he had picked up and turned to go. "And the dressing is not your best," he said.

"It isn't finished," she called. But he had already left the kitchen. Damn the man!

A few minutes later Massu returned. For a moment Marina thought naively that he had come back to apologize. But instead he said, "There is a call for you, Marine, on our main telephone line."

"Oh," she said, wiping her hands on her apron. "Thank you," she added, wondering why Massu himself had come to tell her.

As she preceded him out the door, he said, "Marine, you will please not receive personal calls on that number in the future. The man is a Mr. Barclay, and he did not want a reservation."

Wonderful, she thought. Barclay. She said nothing to Massu, but after she took the phone into the coat room and answered, she could feel her anger at

Massu focusing on Barclay. "Yes," she said with annoyance.

"Marina?" he asked hesitantly.

"Yes, what is it?"

"I, uh, wanted to say hello."

"Look, Barclay, I'm very busy. Today's a special —how did you even know I was here?"

"I remembered the name of the restaurant, Marina. Is that so odd?"

"Well, you forgot I only work nights," she said, surprised by her anger but unable to stop. "Anyway, you also seem to have forgotten that I didn't—that I don't—want to see you again."

"Ah-ha—past tense. Very revealing. The old Freudian slip tells me—"

"That I didn't, don't, and won't want to see you, all right? That sounds pretty clear to me."

There was a silence. Then: "Was what I did so terrible, Marina? You're treating me as if there had never been a thing between us. That just isn't true."

She sighed. "All right, we did have something nice. For a very short time. But it almost doesn't count now, does it? Because you left rather a large fact out. And I'm just tired of that sort of thing, and I don't have time for it. I don't even have time to talk to you right now. Please don't call me again."

After she hung up she closed her eyes and sighed. She wondered if she had been too harsh with Barclay; he was just trying to do things the only way he knew how, and he had made a mistake. Perhaps she was angrier at Massu than Barclay. And perhaps, she thought, she was just tired, fed up with what sud-

87

denly seemed an uphill struggle. Up until now her professional life had been satisfying even if her personal life hadn't. Now she had the sense that her difficulties with Massu would last the summer—while his nephews were going to be here—and perhaps even longer.

The sound of Massu snapping at a busboy brought Marina out of her thoughts, and she let herself out of the coat room. She began to make her way through the dining room—Massu was across the room angrily demonstrating place settings—when she heard the familiar, whiny but commanding, "Marine."

She stopped and turned. "Yes?"

"There was a small fire in the kitchen while you were spending your time in the coat room. If you are going to be so careless that—"

"A fire?" she interrupted. "Is everything all right?"

He gave a Gallic shrug. "Except for a chafing dish sadly burned, perhaps fixable but no longer for us."

"A chafing dish? I'm not even using a chafing dish for today's luncheon."

He shot her a warning look. "You are saying, then—?"

"I'm saying that this morning there have been three people in the kitchen besides you. Me, and your nephews."

"And the fire was caused by Raoul and Alfonse?"

She shrugged. "I don't know. But I know I had nothing to do with it."

"And I know, Mademoiselle Tolchin, that the chefs at this restaurant do not speak back to me."

She raised her chin. "The expression is 'talking back,' and I don't consider it anything other than responding to a rather unjust accusation."

He opened and closed his mouth and then took a deep breath. "Mademoiselle Tolchin, my nephews are here to learn from me. Above all, it is imperative that this be an atmosphere of pleasant learning—no matter what I must do to make it so."

She sighed. "If that's a veiled threat—and it's rather thinly veiled—I think you're making a mistake. You lost one excellent chef this year already. Do you really want to lose another?"

He looked neither disturbed nor surprised by her words. "My nephews are more important to me than the chefs I happen to employ at one moment or another. And it is important for you, Marine, to realize that. Now please, I do not wish to argue. It is an important day, and you are preparing an important meal." He paused. "When we argue, I neglect to tell you how you are an excellent chef. So you will forget what I said about the fire, and I will forget what you said about my losing another chef, and together we will dine on an excellent luncheon after we have served my compatriots."

"I won't forget anything either of us said, Monsieur Massu, and neither will you. So don't bother trying to save the luncheon that way." The color was draining from his face. "I will not be a chef in this restaurant if it means being a scapegoat for the mistakes of your nephews. However, I will not ruin a meal because of an argument. I, too, have a reputation to maintain. And in case you've forgotten, it's my cooking that your friends came to taste. Not yours." She turned and walked back into the kitchen, leaving a nonplussed Massu and a smiling busboy behind.

The luncheon went beautifully; fueled by her anger, Marina prepared a meal that exceeded even her own expectations. But by the end of the day she had made a decision. When she had been walking home, making her way across Fifty-seventh Street in the five o'clock rush-hour traffic, she had realized that her whole body was tensed as if in anticipation of a fight. Her muscles were rigid, her heart was beating quickly, and she couldn't remember one moment of the day in which she hadn't been contemplating one problem or another. She mentally rewrote her arguments with Massu so she always came out the winner, imagined the customers standing up for her and walking out of the restaurant in protest—all sorts of childish fantasies that were also, she realized, her deep, uncensored wishes and sources, also, of great tension.

She realized she was fighting all the time—battling with herself, with others, with ideas and expectations that never seemed to fit reality. For it seemed as if the more she knew what she wanted in any area, the harder everything became. Now that she knew she wanted a deep commitment with a man, now that she knew she wanted to have a family, the only men she met were totally afraid of commitment—or committed to others. And now that she had become a chef—

a goal she had worked for years to achieve, because she loved it and knew she was good at it—the pleasures were quickly souring. And she knew it was because she was struggling too hard, fighting against the grain when there was no need to fight.

And she knew then that she had a once-in-a-lifetime chance to go for something she really wanted, and to do it in the only way that was possible: by herself. She would leave the city, where the men were impossible and the unpleasantnesses of her job far exceeded its rewards. She would open up Windy Hill as her own, a gourmet restaurant-inn that would be close enough to New York so people could drive there from the city for lunch or dinner, and lovely enough so that they'd want to stay the night or a week or forever. And at least then she'd be running her life independently, doing exactly what she wanted without depending on anyone else. And though she would in a sense be putting more emphasis on her professional life than her emotional life, she felt it made sense at this point. She wasn't afraid of being alone, and if she did meet a man, fall in love, and have children, she would already have set herself up in a job in which she could spend most of her time with her children.

The moment she got home to her apartment, she called Dan.

He was happy to hear from her, but when she told him her decision, there was only silence.

"Are you there?" she asked.

"Yes. I'm just surprised," he said. "I had thought we were going to talk about it."

"Well, the decision kind of came to me in a flash. Work went pretty badly, and a whole combination of things made me realize that there's nothing holding me in the city. But that's sort of negative reasoning. Basically I'm taking a chance that's only going to happen once, and I'm really happy."

"What does Alex think?"

She closed her eyes. She had completely—and conveniently—forgotten her brother. "I . . . uh, don't know." She shook her head. "I can't believe it, but I completely put him out of my mind." She paused. "You don't sound very enthusiastic, you know."

"To be honest, Marina, that's because I'm not. You'll be broke and out of your mind in two months."

"Thanks so much for your confidence, Dan. You're a true friend."

"Marina, if anyone could do what you plan, it would be you. But I just don't think it's possible. And I wouldn't *be* a friend if I didn't tell you how I felt." There was an uncomfortable silence, which he finally broke. "What are your plans?" he asked quietly.

"Well, I thought I'd go up this weekend—I'm going to insist that Massu give me the time off—and then I can see exactly what needs to be done."

Dan sighed. "Look, I'll come along, okay? And don't say anything about not wanting to spend the weekend together. Obviously you know what I'd like —what we'd both like, on one level. But you also know I'm not going to force anything. You'll need either me or somebody else who knows about houses and pipes and electricity and all that. I'll bring up some of my old camping equipment." His voice softened as he spoke his next words. "It could be incredibly nice, Marina. Sleeping under the stars, in the moonlight . . ."

She sighed, her dreams of the night coming back to her—of Dan as an immensely exciting lover—and she realized that her dreams had taken place at Windy Hill, among the wildflowers on the gentle slope below the inn.

"Then come," she said, throwing doubt to the wind.

Surprisingly Marina had no trouble getting Massu to let her off for the weekend; perhaps, she thought, he sensed her newfound determination not to be stepped on. Perhaps he even sensed—or hoped—she was about to give notice. But she did want to have at least one more look at Windy Hill before making her break with L'Aigle d'Or final.

Saturday morning was beautiful, with the long rays of the early morning sun casting an amber glow over all the meadows and mountains along the roads leading to Windy Hill.

Dan seemed more enthusiastic about the prospect of going to the country than he had the first time, as if his memories of the wilderness had finally reawakened. He pointed out rare birds and trees along the way, spotted deer Marina could only occasionally see, recounted adventures he had had in the woods, along rivers, even in the air when he had hang-glided. Hearing him talk with such enthusiasm about something he loved so much made Marina confident that perhaps he hadn't changed as much as she had thought. He had buried this aspect of himself under layers of attributes he thought he needed in his career, but his love for the wild had never, in fact, disappeared.

As they started the drive up the long, winding road leading to Windy Hill, Dan turned to Marina with a gleam in his dark eyes. "You know, I didn't come on this trip just for the sake of the two of us, or just to help you. It was for myself as well." He raised a brow. "Much as I don't want to admit it—for a variety of reasons—I suddenly feel as if I want all this—or need all this—the fresh air, the mountains, the woods—as much as you say you do."

She smiled. "The big bad city finally getting to you, then?"

He frowned. "I think it's been getting to me for years without my realizing it. When I was married to Ellie and we went on vacations, it was always somewhere exotic, expensive, and extravagant. We spent a ton of money, did too much drinking and sightseeing, then came back exhausted and hung over. When I became single again"—he winked—"a slightly more positive way to look at being divorced —I went on the same sort of trip by myself. And it sounds corny, but I've missed the pleasures of just walking through the woods, and fishing, even just looking up from the grass at a cloudless sky."

She smiled. "I hope you take the time to do some of those things this weekend. Knowing you, you'll feel so guilty about taking time off from your work in the city that the only cloudless sky you'll see will be through a hole in a roof that you're patching."

He narrowed his eyes and looked at her with a warmth that made her heart race. "I'm more than ready to grab pleasure when it comes along, Marina," he said, capturing her in his gaze. "I came up to be with you"—he inhaled deeply—"a pleasure that has yet to be fully explored. And to do some of the things I miss. If I wanted to play with plaster and plumbing and paint, I could fix up my apartment back in town."

She frowned as they pulled up to the rutted driveway and she saw that she had apparently improved the structure of Windy Hill in her mind since she had last seen it. It was much, much worse than she remembered, and there was an enormous amount of work to be done. "Now I feel guilty," she said. "Because I really do need your help getting the water started and figuring out what needs to be done. Look at it—it's hopeless!"

He put a hand on her knee and looked into her eyes. "Relax," he commanded. "We certainly know each other well enough not to have to tiptoe around each other's feelings. If I get tired of doing something —which I can't imagine—I'll tell you," His voice softened. "The way you've made it clear that you're not ready to make love with me."

She looked into his eyes and then away, wanting to contradict him but knowing it was better—and safer—not to.

They unloaded the car, which was packed full with camping equipment, sleeping bags, food, coolers, water, and clothes. "You've brought enough to stay for weeks," Marina marveled.

He smiled. "Wishful thinking. Listen, as long as the sun's out and we're sweating like animals, let's take a swim before we get started." He paused, a gleam in his eye. "Did you bring a suit?" he asked.

"Sure. Didn't you?"

He winked. "I never lie. Yes, I did. But I was just hoping . . ."

She punched him in the shoulder. "You're impossible," she said with a laugh. "I'll see you out by the creek." And she took her bag into one of the downstairs bathrooms and changed into her swimsuit, a small blue bikini that matched the blue of her eyes. Then she took a bottle of suntan lotion, two towels, and a big old blanket and carried them out through the musty commons room and outside.

Outdoors was pure delight, with the fragrance of wildflowers released by the sun and the wind as Marina walked through the tall grass. The strip of forest that separated the field from the creek had thickened with young green saplings and hardy vines over the years, and the old path that led to the best spot by the water was now completely obscured. But she made her way through the woods, so familiarly scented with the heady fragrance of honeysuckle, to the area her family had cleared years before. The sandy beach was as warm and clear and sunny as ever, with thick sprays of sky-blue forget-me-nots edging its gentle banks.

Marina spread the blanket out flat on the sand and then walked to the water's edge, where the rocks were cool and wet and slippery. She heard the rustling of branches behind her, and as she turned, Dan emerged from the woods. He looked magnificent, his tall, lean body clad only in a small red swimsuit. He was lithe and muscular and tanned, his broad shoulders and flat stomach tapering to narrow hips and long, lean thighs. His tanned skin was darkened by fine dark hairs covering his chest and thighs, and Marina could only marvel at how he had kept in shape over the years.

As he came across the sand, he looked at Marina with undisguised desire, his gaze traveling slowly along her body, making her feel self-conscious and stirred with wanting at one and the same time.

He came up to her, his eyes never leaving hers, and put his warm, strong hands at the curve of her waist, his thumbs arching down over the soft skin just above her bikini bottom. "I know what you want," he murmured, his eyes dark. "You want to keep everything simple, Marina, to keep everything easy to understand." As his fingers splayed down over her hips, their gentle but urgent pressure quickened the beating of her heart. "The problem, Marina, is that things aren't always as easy as we want them to be." He pulled her close, and the feel of his firm body, warmed by the sun and desire, naked except for one small piece of fabric, sent a searing rush of yearning through her. "As far as I know," he said quietly, his voice as soft as the breeze, "there would be nothing easier in the world than making love with you right now, just taking you into my arms and—"

"No," she whispered, shaking her head, though

her eyes were heavy with need and her voice was thick with desire. "That isn't what I want." She was suddenly aware of the pressure of his hips against hers, skin against warm skin she had never felt, the knowledge that his expert hands tight around her hips could coax her to any action at that moment, any pleasure. "I . . ." She had to force her voice up through layers of thick need. "It isn't that I don't want you," she said. "You know that, and you know I don't even have to tell you—"

"I can feel it," he whispered. "As you can feel me. Now come," he said quietly. "Not to make love if you don't want to. Just come." She looked up into his eyes, caught by their warmth, and as her lips parted to speak, he leaned down and swept her into his arms, one arm behind her back and a hand warm against her upper thighs.

A moment later, she lay on the blanket, Dan half-sitting and half-lying beside her, looking down at her with deep desire. "I understand what you've been saying," he said quietly, taking the bottle of suntan lotion and pouring some out into his hand.

She propped herself up on her elbows. "But what?" she asked. "I can hear there's a 'but' in there somewhere." She winked. "I know you better than you might think."

"No ifs, ands, or buts, Marina. Here. Lie back and I'll put some of this on you."

She laughed. "Forget it. What kind of fool do you think I am?"

"Meaning what?" he asked, dabbing some lotion on to her thigh and beginning to slowly rub it in.

The touch sent a tremor of warm pleasure through her, and as his hand kneaded its way along her inner thigh, she felt as if she were melting into a state of pleasure she'd never be able to give up.

"Do you want me to stop?" he asked, leaning over and starting with another hand on her other thigh.

"Yes," she said thickly.

"Why?" he asked. "It looks as if it might feel good. I was hoping you'd do the same for me."

She remembered the way his hard thighs felt under her touch, the eagerness of his response, the strength of his arousal. "Not very likely," she said, smiling.

"Why do you want me to stop?" he asked as he worked his fingers upward, over her bikini bottom and then along its upper edge, over the flat of her stomach and up towards her breasts. "Why do you want me to stop?" he whispered, sliding down next to her and urging a thigh between her own.

"Because it feels too good," she answered hoarsely. "And I won't want to stop . . . I don't want to stop."

"Oh, Marina," he moaned, moving on top of her, stroking her flesh and parting her thighs with his own. The impact was thrilling, and Marina roved her hands hungrily along his flesh, up and down the backs of his hard thighs, wanting him closer, closer, as close as only full lovemaking could bring them.

"Please," she breathed, each movement of his kindling her desire, arousing her to greater need.

"Please what?" he whispered.

She wanted to say, Please take me; she wanted to moan, Please love me; but she knew that what she had to say, so untruthfully, was Please stop. But she said nothing as his coaxing fingers made her tremble with desire and clutch him with desperate, breathless craving.

"Tell me the time is right," he urged. "Tell me you want me," he rasped, "and I'll give you pleasure you've never imagined."

"Oh Dan," she breathed. "I want you. I want you so much. But—"

She felt his body tense, his movements slow, a long intake of breath he seemed to hold forever.

"I want you so much," she whispered. "But I just can't make love with you now . . . not yet." She sighed, her body slowing, unwinding, descending. "I'm sorry," she said slowly. "I didn't mean to let go like that. But when we came so close and I realized . . ." Her voice trailed off.

He sighed against her neck and raised his head. "Marina," he said quietly, "your responses are so full. It's obvious that we're right for each other, that we'd be so good together . . . that you want me as much as I want you." He reached up and stroked her forehead, damp from exertion, with the back of his hand. "I'm reacting to the way you talk to me without words—with your lips, your eyes, your breathing, your hunger that I feel in every kiss. You know I wouldn't even touch you if you didn't want me to. But Marina, what I feel as your body moves with mine is that you want me to love you—to make love to you and make up for all the time we've lost, all the times we've missed."

"I do," she whispered. She captured his eyes with

hers, wanting him to feel the pain of resistance as much as she did. "But I just can't." She sighed. "For me there's a big difference between making love and coming within a breath of making love. It doesn't have to do with morals, or the length of time I've known someone, or anything other than my knowing we're going somewhere—that the relationship is real and solid and promising and . . . different, I guess, than ours is."

His eyes were filled with regret as he quietly asked, "Are you talking about marriage?"

She shook her head. "No. But something—a potential—which I don't feel you feel."

He frowned. "I care so much about you, Marina. I have for years."

"But not in this way," she said. "You seem to be a very, very different person in some ways. And we can't count on the past to carry us through." She paused.

They looked into each other's eyes in silence, and then Marina spoke again. "In a sense we're both counting on the past. You're thinking of our friendship and translating it into something else, and I keep expecting you to be someone you're not."

He frowned. "I can't change, Marina," he said. "You bring out something in me I thought was lost, but it's not really me anymore. It's wonderful to be here, it's wonderful to be in your arms in this incredibly beautiful place. But in the back of my mind I feel as if I've run away from the world for a few hours or a few days."

She sighed. "I know," she said quietly as she lay

her cheek against his and he settled his arms more comfortably around her. She wrapped her arms around him and closed her eyes, warmed by the sun and Dan's nearness, lulled by the gentle calls of the birds.

A few moments later Dan shifted and leaned up on one elbow, and Marina looked up at him.

"This isn't going to work," he said. "I'm sorry, Marina, but I can't lie here with my arms around you like this. My mind races on to various incredibly exciting possibilities, and if we keep this up my body is going to be making some pretty rough demands." Suddenly his face tightened, and he swore. "Damn," he added softly.

"What? What's the matter?" she asked, sitting up.

He sat up cross-legged and shook his head, a half-smile on his handsome face. "I don't know what made me think of this"—he grinned—"maybe 'rough demands' had something to do with it—but I had a message to call Ellie—my secretary said it sounded pretty important—and I completely forgot."

"You'd better call, then." She frowned. "It isn't like you to forget something like that."

He looked doubtful. "I'm not so sure of that," he said. "Ellie has called me so many times for 'urgent' reasons. And they're always unimportant." He looked wistful. "You know, I would call her any time of the day or night if I knew it was just because she wanted to talk. But the 'urgency' of her reasons can get a little annoying at times, and I've started unconsciously to forget to call her back."

"Have you told her?" Marina asked. "Maybe if she knew . . ."

"I've tried. But she always insists she's calling for a reason, and I don't want to press the issue. She's going through a big change, actually—becoming a lot more independent than she ever was, a lot more aware of what she wants out of life. It was almost as if when we were married, she forced me into smothering her, and I did."

Marina frowned. "In what way, exactly?"

"I was totally responsible for everything, from making all the money and choosing our friends and how we spent our time to the tiniest of decisions, like what we were going to eat for dinner. Ellie wasn't like that—to that extent—until we married, and it's taken the divorce to get her out of it." He sighed. "But listen, I really ought to call her. Why don't we go through the house and see what I need in the way of supplies today, and then we can drive in to town and buy whatever I need, and I can call Ellie from there."

"Great. What kind of supplies, though?"

"Well, it would be nice to get the water started, for one thing, so at the very least I'm going to need some washers and faucets, maybe some new pipes." He looked at her. "That is," he said slowly, "if you had the electricity turned on."

She smiled. "Yes, after I first came up here. And I ordered a phone. But I'm surprised at you; I thought you'd consider even getting electricity or a phone a hasty move. Since I haven't absolutely decided about opening Windy Hill or not."

"I've decided one thing for sure," he said, reaching out and gently running a hand along her cheek. "Now that I've met you again, and now that I've seen the incredible beauty of these woods and fields and this creek, I'm not giving any of it up."

They looked into each other's eyes, and a warm, light breeze carried the heavy scent of honeysuckle to their senses.

"You are so beautiful," he said softly. "Right now your eyes are the color of the forget-me-nots and the sky, and I feel as if all of this—the scents, the feel of it—is part of you." She smiled, entranced. "And for the first time, Marina, I can see why you'll do almost anything to keep this place. And I'm going to help you as much as I can," he said. "But on one condition," he added.

"What's that?"

"That you stop making it impossible for me to think about anything but taking you in my arms and making love." He smiled. "Look the other way, maybe. Or draw on a mustache or something. Shave your head."

She laughed. "I'll try to look as terrible as I can," she promised, her fingers crossed behind her back.

Having Dan go through the house checking on what work needed to be done was like having a contractor and his entire team of men at work. He turned on the water, at first getting a great brown gush, and figured out which washers, faucets, and pipes needed replacing; checked a lot of the wiring; and checked over some of the more serious holes in the roof. At first Marina felt foolish and annoyingly helpless—having grown up in the city, she knew next to nothing about what Dan was doing. But she was determined to learn; after all, maintenance would be costly if she had to bring in people to make repairs constantly. And in addition, the acquisition of that sort of knowledge was exactly what she had had in mind when she had decided to go out on her own and run Windy Hill by herself. It was the kind of basic skill she could use forever, and as she began asking Dan questions about what he was doing, she started to look forward to the whole Windy Hill experience more than ever. It would be an adventure in self-sufficiency, a strength she had never tested in her entire life.

Dan shut off the water and took apart several fittings in the cellar and upstairs, and soon he and Marina were off to town.

The town was lovely, though more built up than Marina remembered, with a modern grouping of stores a short distance from the main, more old-fashioned part of town. Marina loved watching Dan talking with the old man who ran the hardware store; they talked about fishing and hunting for ten minutes before Dan mentioned what he was there for, and by the time Dan was ready to leave, the old man was saying how he hoped to see Dan again, maybe go fishing with him up at the creek.

As Marina and Dan walked down the street, Dan smiled and shook his head. "What a pleasure," he marveled. "In the city we would have had to take a number and wait on a line thirty people long, the clerk would have been surly, and the store wouldn't have even had what we needed."

Marina smiled, pleased that the atmosphere of the mountains was reaching Dan.

They went to the Village Restaurant, the town's only eating place, for a good, inexpensive lunch, and then Dan called Ellie from a phone at the restaurant. As he talked, Marina waited at the table with a local newspaper spread out before her. Though she was interested in it—especially in the level of detail that never appeared in New York City papers—she wasn't really concentrating. For she kept thinking about Dan and Ellie, how odd it was that she was with Dan now, that both marriages were over, that so many things had changed. And she felt—at least hoped—that Dan himself was changing once again, becoming more like his old self as he spent more time with her. It made sense, really, that this would be so, for he was no longer forced to play a certain kind of role with Ellie, and he was in the type of place he had once loved and thrived in.

When Dan returned to the booth, he was smiling. "Amazing," he said as he sat down across from her.

"What?"

He shook his head. "It's just amazing how much better Ellie and I get along now that we're apart."

Marina raised a brow and looked at him mock-suspiciously. "Going to start up with her again?" she asked.

He widened his eyes. "Definitely not. Never. This is the only way we can really like each other." He reached across the table and took Marina's hand.

"It's over between me and Ellie," he said quietly, looking into her eyes. "And if you have any guilt about the past, put it out of your mind." He paused. "You know, now I look back at all the times we were together and I see how I hid my feelings about you even from myself, but there's still no reason to feel guilty." He sighed. "But talking to Ellie made me realize something, Marina." He let go of her hand and took a sip of coffee.

"What?" she asked.

"I care about you so much," he said quietly, "and I don't want to lead you on, to make promises that aren't true. I know we've talked about it, but Ellie made me realize how important it is to be clear."

Marina frowned. "Why? What did she say?"

"Well, I told her I was up here with you, and what we were doing with Windy Hill and all." Marina smiled inwardly at his use of the word "we," but his next words dispelled her optimism. "She asked if it was serious between the two of us," he continued, "and when I hedged, she said she'd be very surprised to find you in some sort of casual fling with me, especially after all this time." He sighed. "I don't consider this exactly a casual fling, Marina, but I don't want to be anything other than honest."

"What you're being," she interrupted, "is just like a lot of men who think that 'honesty' is great. I don't know how it is that all of you are so sure of the future. I don't know how to say this, but don't consider what you've said as a guarantee against hurt feelings or disappointment or anything else. And don't think of it as any great positive reflection on you, either, because that's the kind of statement that makes me want to stop seeing someone."

He looked at her steadily. "Do you want us to stop seeing each other, then?" he asked.

She looked at him, wondering what he would do and say if she said yes. But she answered the only way she wanted to: "No," she said. "But I just think —at least for the rest of the weekend—that we should keep a certain distance." She sighed. "You know, not advance things any more than they already are," she said vaguely, suddenly aware of the people sitting in back of her, who had stopped talking at some point she hadn't noticed.

Dan looked into her eyes and took her hand in both of his. "Lying in your arms this morning was pure heaven, Marina. Just being near you—almost as much as anything else—is a pleasure I wouldn't voluntarily give up, ever. If it has to go on as you've suggested, at a certain distance, I don't think I'll be able to help you with Windy Hill as I had envisioned —on weekends over the summer, say"—he frowned —"and it isn't out of some teenage male need or blind lust, but because my picture of our being together and working on something together also involves making love. And I think yours does, too."

She looked into his eyes and said nothing, and looked away. At times—as now—he was clear and wonderful and positive. But if he couldn't give up the idea—even if it were only to relieve his fear of commitment—that the relationship had no future, she knew she'd never be able to open herself to him emotionally as she so much wanted to.

CHAPTER SIX

Over the rest of the day Dan and Marina worked long and hard, then picnicked on delicious food and worked again until it was too dark and too late and they were too tired to work anymore. Each fantasized about lovemaking under the stars; each tried not to look at the other's body, tanned and firm from working; each wondered what would happen if even a kiss were attempted. But each knew also that another confrontation might tip the delicate balance of the relationship in the wrong direction. And so that night they slept apart, arms around each other but in separate sleeping bags, and they were both so exhausted that neither awakened once during the night.

The next day they worked separately—Dan in the cellar, Marina sweeping and scraping and cleaning indoors. And by the end of the day both were amazed at how much they had accomplished and how different the inn already looked.

As they were carrying their bags out through the commons room, Dan turned to Marina and softly said, "Wait a minute." He put down his bags and took hers and set them down, then stepped forward and put his hands on her waist.

Immediately she felt unwelcome warmth, unbidden desire as his fingers found the flesh beneath her shirt. And when she looked into his deep brown eyes, so soft with affection, deep and dark with desire, her lips parted.

"Marina," he murmured, half-smiling. "The weekend is over, and if I don't do this now, I'll never forgive—" They had come closer as he had spoken, and their lips met in a surge of unbridled heat before his words were finished. He parted her lips with his as his tongue found the willing sweetness of her mouth, and she moaned with need as she ran her hands along his back, whose warm flesh she had touched, whose weight she had felt and wanted completely, whose skin she wanted to rake in the blaze of passion she ached for. His lips roved down her neck and he raked his teeth along her collarbone, sending a thrill of pleasure-pain and liquid desire through her whole body.

When he raised his head and gazed at her, his eyes were cloudy with desire, heavy-lidded with pleasure and need. "If I don't stop now . . ." he whispered huskily.

Her breath was coming too quickly to speak, and she was glad; for she was afraid she would say, Don't stop—I want you so much. Instead she said nothing, looking into his eyes and letting her breathing slow, her pulse try to come back to normal.

"Somehow, Marina," he whispered. "I promise you we're going to make love."

She looked into his eyes and silently hoped he was right.

Late that afternoon, after Dan dropped Marina off at her apartment, she felt an unexpected letdown, a sense of incompleteness she couldn't shake even when she awakened the next morning. She missed him; and she was suddenly swept with regret thinking about the weekend, annoyed with herself for having made things more difficult than they had to be.

But she didn't have time to be distracted by her feelings. For on the way back to New York she had decided once and for all to quit her job and open Windy Hill. And if she was going to make any money out of it this summer, she couldn't waste a moment more.

The first thing she did on Monday morning was to try to reach Alex. She had put off discussing her tentative plans with him because she knew how negative he'd be, but now she had no choice. He wasn't home, though, and she left a message on his answering machine to call her; anything more detailed, or any mention of Windy Hill, was apt to set him off in a fury.

Then she dialed the number of L'Aigle d'Or; better to call now than wait to face Massu's certain irrational behavior in person. When he answered, she told him straight out: she was giving two weeks' notice.

There was silence. Then: "You are joining another restaurant?"

She smiled. "No. Opening my own, as a matter of fact."

Silence again. Then a deafening barrage of French, only some of which—"betrayal," "treacherous," "the worst of luck"—Marina could understand. "Marine, you will not come back to cook your last meal here," he hissed. "I do not wish you in the kitchen. My nephews and I will manage."

"Monsieur Massu, I really would be happy to come in," she said, filled with something akin to generosity of spirit now that she wasn't his slave. She could only begin to imagine the sure chaos that would ensue with Raoul, Alfonse and Massu trying even to boil an egg.

"Good-bye, Marine. That is all I have to say. I will read about you in the newspapers, perhaps, and know that you betrayed me."

He hung up, and she shook her head. He certainly hadn't made the parting graceful, but at least now she had a two-week jump on her own business.

The phone rang, and Marina answered it.

"Marina, it's Ellie." There was a slight pause during which each woman wondered how awkward the other thought it was that they were finally in touch again after all this time; but each was glad it had happened. "How are you?" Ellie asked.

"Great. I've been meaning to call you," Marina

said, realizing that only a few weeks ago the words wouldn't have been true.

"Especially now, I'll bet," Ellie said. "I heard all about Windy Hill, Marina, and I think it's great. So how about lunch? I'd like to talk."

They arranged to meet that day, and after making a few more calls Marina left to meet her old friend.

They had arranged to meet outdoors at a midtown restaurant with a sidewalk café, and when Marina arrived, she almost didn't see Ellie. The woman looked vastly different, and much prettier. Her light brown hair, which had once been straight and almost prim-looking, was now curly and short, and her clothes were much more stylish and flattering. But as Marina walked toward Ellie, she realized that the main difference was in Ellie's whole demeanor: waiting alone in a busy restaurant for a friend, the Ellie of the old days would have managed to look extremely ill at ease even to the most uninterested passerby. Now she looked perfectly relaxed, and when she saw Marina, her blue eyes lit up and she called out loudly, "Well, hi!" paying no attention to the fact that several people turned, thinking she was talking to them.

When Marina sat down, Ellie summoned the waiter, ordered another drink for herself and one for Marina, and then turned to Marina with a sparkle in her eyes. "So we won't pretend we're getting together by chance, okay? Tell me everything, beginning with when did you start seeing Dan?"

Marina laughed. Ellie's love for gossip had always been strong. "Oh, a few weeks ago. He was my grandmother's attorney, and when she died, I had to go to his office for the reading of the will."

Ellie's eyes widened. "Tatiana? The one you really liked?" Marina nodded. "Gee, that's terrible. So this Windy Hill was the thing you thought she had sold?"

"Yes. I guess Dan told you something about it."

"Sure," Ellie said enthusiastically. "I can pump anything out of anyone—even Dan. And I think it sounds fantastic. I have only two things to say about it, though: One, I'm working on *East Side Living* magazine, and—"

Marina smiled. "You're working? You of the 'what else are husbands for' school of thought?"

Ellie shrugged. "What husband? And it's great, anyway. I've never been happier. And that's the second thing: Do it no matter what anyone says. It's your big chance now, no matter what Mr. Conservative-don't-do-it-Dan says."

"Did he tell you he thought I shouldn't?" Marina asked.

Ellie shook her head. "Uh-uh. But I know him. The way he used to worry about money and working, you'd have thought we had ten houses we had to pay mortgages on. And Marina, we were renting an apartment we could afford really easily."

Marina looked into her friend's eyes. "I gather he just felt a great responsibility for you . . . in a kind of old-fashioned way."

Ellie sighed. "Yes. Well, I shouldn't criticize, I guess. God knows I drove him to it." She shrugged. "It's funny. Now that I've gone out and begun working and meeting people, I've really started to realize how crazy I must have driven Dan. And for a while I thought, Gee, maybe we should get back together now that things are going well." She sighed. "But it wasn't what I really wanted; it was just that I was afraid Dan was going to be it—you know, the love of my life," She smiled. "But I've just met someone, Marina, and he seems pretty great."

Marina smiled. "That's wonderful."

"Yeah, well, we'll see. But listen, what *is* with you and Dan? Is it love-of-your-life time for you, or what?" She narrowed her eyes and smiled. "You know, I *could* get upset about the fact that if you two are really crazy about each other, it must have been true back then when we were all friends. But I'm not going to even think about it because it's just silly." The look in her eyes, though, belied her words, and Marina felt obliged to set her straight.

"It wasn't anything like what you might be thinking," Marina said. "We both always considered each other good friends, and that was it."

"And now?" Ellie looked down at her drink and then into Marina's eyes. "I think Dan is a great, great person, Marina. I messed things up with him and we were wrong for each other. But I can see the two of you really working things out. If you don't push him."

Marina smiled. "This is terrible; I feel as if we're plotting some terrible deed or conspiring on a crime. But tell me—what specifically shouldn't I push him on?"

Ellie looked almost grim. "Anything," she said flatly. "From what I hear him saying these days, he's

115

still running scared from any woman who might have possibilities."

Marina nodded. "I know. He seems to spend a lot of time in singles bars."

Ellie waved the idea away. "Just an act," she said. "Forget it. But learn from it, too. Because part of him believes that's the kind of woman he wants." She sighed. "Basically, if you want him you'll just have to convince him he wants you—seriously—but so he doesn't realize he's being convinced."

Marina looked at her friend and smiled conspiratorially, but deep down she didn't like the implications of what Ellie was saying. For much as Ellie had changed, she was still loyal to the concept of snaring the man, and Marina didn't altogether like the feeling of being part of a plan.

Yet the best thing that had come out of the whole conversation with Ellie was another feeling, something she had realized as Ellie was talking. Deep down she wasn't worried that Dan had changed or that he was someone too superficial or shallow to be interested in; no, it was easy to see that he had just had a natural reaction to having been part of a marriage which both partners were desperately trying to break away from emotionally.

When the lunch was over Marina and Ellie promised to keep in touch, but each knew she probably wouldn't call the other, at least for a while; the get-together had been a rite of passage of sorts, an occasion to mark a change. Now each woman would go on her way, not to reestablish contact until another change took place.

When Marina got home there was a message from Alex that he had returned her call. Marina marveled at how, through his tone of voice and few words, even on a tape Alex had been able to convey reluctance and hostility.

When she called him back, just to lighten the mood Marina joked about his message. But she could hear he wasn't even smiling.

"What's going on?" was all he said.

"Well, I've . . . I've decided to open Windy Hill," Marina said simply, knowing that no matter how she broke the news, Alex would be furious.

"You what!" he cried. "What the hell are you talking about?"

"Just what I said. I'm opening Windy Hill as a restaurant, mainly, but also as an inn."

"You can't," he said, his voice flat.

"Sorry, Alex; I can. Under the terms of the will, I would need your agreement only to sell, not to open it up."

He was silent for a few moments. "You don't know anything about running a place like that," he said. "It takes much more money than you have. And if you're undercapitalized, the whole place will go under and you won't be able to repay whatever loans you do manage to get. Then you'll have to sell the property low to raise cash, and there goes my investment."

"Your investment?" she asked. "Just what investment is that? I don't recall your having invested any money in Windy Hill when you were growing up. If you remember, Alex, it belonged to Tatiana Alexeva.

And I watched her and helped her run it for years, even if you didn't."

"Your remarks cut me to the quick, Marina. The point is that while I haven't invested money in the property, it is half mine now. And I have a right to see that my half isn't jeopardized."

"Why?" she asked. "So you can sell it to some real estate speculator? Uh-uh. That wasn't what Tatiana had in mind, and it's definitely not what I have in mind." She paused. "Naturally it would be nice if you wanted to go in on this with me. It *is* what Tatiana wanted. But since that's too much to hope for and she was probably dreaming anyway, I'm just calling to let you know I'm doing it. If you'd like to come see what I'm doing with the place, fine. If not, fine."

"I'll think about it," he said and hung up.

Marina swore softly and picked up the phone to call Dan. Knowing Alex, there was a good chance he would find some way, legal or otherwise, of preventing her from carrying out her plans. And she knew she had only made the situation worse by mentioning Tatiana's name, as Alex invariably grew angrier instantly whenever he thought Marina was using Tatiana to prove a point.

"Marina," Dan said after she had been put through by his secretary.

"Hi. Listen, is there any way Alex—well, first of all, how are you?"

He laughed. "Just fine. Great, after the weekend."

She smiled. "Good."

"Now what's the trouble? Did you tell Alex?"

"Well, yes," she said. "And not in the best way possible, I guess. He's less than happy, let's say."

She heard Dan sigh. "All right, look, I'll talk to him. Remember I was against this whole thing to begin with, too. I'll probably be able to calm him down, answer his objections. What else? How are the permits downtown going?"

"Well, I'm about to begin. I had lunch with Ellie today instead, and—"

"Ellie?" he asked.

She laughed. "Yes, Ellie. The former Ellie Sommers. Remember?"

He was silent.

"What's the matter?" she asked.

"I'm not sure I like the idea of a new girl friend talking to a former wife. My reputation as, uh . . . well, my reputation is at stake," he said and laughed.

"Don't worry, you came out unscathed. But anyway, I thought I'd get it over with with Alex and then start on the permits."

"I have a better idea," he said. "Why don't I take care of Alex and the permits, and you go up and get some of the renovation really going, okay? I'll come up on the weekend and do some more work on the plumbing, and by then Alex should be calmed down and the very slow wheels of justice should be moving on your permits."

"That sounds great. But I don't know if I want you so—"

"What?" he asked. "You don't want me so what?"

"Well, Windy Hill is something I'm working on by

119

myself. Doing as independently as possible. And already you're doing so much."

"I'm doing it because I want to," he said. "Believe me, Marina, I'm overloaded enough that I don't offer help like this unless I very much want to do it. As I do."

She sighed. "And what, then, is the difference between the kind of responsibility you're taking on now and the kind you took with Ellie?" she asked.

"Every difference in the world," he said. "Believe me." He paused. "So go up, take care of as much as you can, and I'll see you Friday night."

She smiled. "Okay, Friday night, then. You remember the way?"

"I could never forget the way to one of the most delightful places I've ever been," he said. "Or the way to the new home of one of the most compelling women I've ever met."

She laughed. "Let's hope you still think that after we've worked on the place for a while and I'm covered with plaster and paint."

"Oh, Marina," he murmured. "How little you know sometimes. Just go and get to work, and I'll see you Friday."

Marina drove up to Windy Hill the next day, with two books she had bought on renovating old houses, some cookbooks and her manual from L'Aigle d'Or, and lots of clothes. She knew the only way to get anything done was to throw herself into it, commit herself totally, and one action she'd taken in this vein—one that made her nervous but that she knew was essentially right—was to transfer almost all her savings into her checking account. She'd need to buy an enormous number of essentials just to make Windy Hill livable, and it all cost money.

When she arrived at Windy Hill, experiencing for the first time the arduousness of trying to get her ten-year-old car up the rutted mountain road, she had a moment of panic: was she doing the right thing by trying to go out on her own in so many ways? She had turned her life upside down in the morning by quitting her job; and now, standing alone as she looked at the dilapidated structure of Windy Hill, she wondered what had ever possessed her to think she could run it by herself. And she hadn't even given a thought to the winter. What then? She had a picture of herself huddled in front of the big Colonial-era fireplace, all alone and wrapped in blankets, and she wondered whether she had ever felt as lonely or as cold as she would feel when that time came.

But then she had a picture of herself as a success, with people from miles around coming to Windy Hill, one of the thirteen five-star restaurants in New York State. People would read about her cooking in the newspaper, as Jean-Pierre Massu had predicted, and she would at least have escaped the wearing and pointless anxieties and egotistical men of the city and made a life for herself.

There was something, however, in the fantasy that disturbed her, that just didn't sit right. And she realized that what was keeping her from being thrilled with the adventure, fueled by the unpredictability of it all, was that she was thinking only in terms of success and failure, and then only in financial terms.

And she didn't feel right about that, because she wasn't going out on a limb for money or professional fame; she was doing it because she wanted to take a chance on doing something she loved and knew she did well. And *that* was something she could be excited about. And the thought made the sight of Windy Hill much, much less daunting. It would be an adventure—nothing more, nothing less, with no promises and no guarantees.

Marina worked herself to near-exhaustion over the next few days, and though the work was hard— or perhaps because it was hard—at the end of each day she felt wonderful as she flopped into bed and slept completely soundly. She worked only on the first floor of the inn—the rooms upstairs were relatively unimportant compared with the rooms she'd need for the restaurant part of the business—and it was especially satisfying because even though the work was monotonous, she could see wonderful results at the end of each day, even at the end of each hour: she scraped the walls of their old, once-beautiful paper and measured them for new; she swept and mopped and cleaned until there was no more glass, dust, or dirt on the floor; she measured the kitchen for new appliances and had a refrigerator and freezer delivered on the second day she was there; she bought a few pieces of furniture—a table, an old brass bed, some chairs—at a local antique/junk shop, and made a small part of the first floor livable.

Glaziers began putting in new windows, and by Friday night the first floor of the inn was almost unrecognizable.

All week as Marina worked, rested, ate, and slept, her thoughts were on Dan. She missed him terribly, though she had just seen him. But each time she spoke with him—when he'd call her late at night to say he was thinking of her, or she'd call him during the day with a question—his voice was so full of affection, so intimate, that she felt almost as if he were with her. Once, after she had hung up, she realized she had been about to say "I love you" in the most casual of ways, and she smiled. For the feeling had slipped in while she was unaware, come into her heart and body and soul and filled her with love for this man she was really just beginning to know again.

Friday night, when she heard the sound of Dan's car coming up the driveway, her heart raced in anticipation. She wanted to tell him everything that had happened that week, to know all he had felt during his, but most of all she yearned to be in his arms, to share kisses unlike any she had ever known as he awakened needs that only he could kindle, only he could satisfy . . . if she would let him.

She stood on the veranda and watched him walk up the driveway; he was handsome and lithe in the pale moonlight, like a vision from a dream.

He raced up the steps and embraced her fiercely, his hold firm and strong. "Marina," he murmured. He slowly shook his head. "As beautiful in the moonlight as in the day." He leaned down and brushed his lips against hers, and she responded instantaneously, fueled by the long week's wait, long nights of thinking about his lips, his flesh, his desire.

Gently he drew his head back and gazed into her eyes. "I thought about you all week," he said softly. "Every day. Every night." He looked up at the moon —it was bright and full—and again at Marina. "Come," he said, putting an arm around her waist. "Let's walk for a bit. It's too beautiful a night to spend inside."

She smiled in agreement, and they descended the steps and walked out into the tall grasses of the lawn. The light was almost as bright as the light of day, and as Marina looked up at Dan, at his strong, handsome profile, she was filled with love once more, filled with wonderment that after all these years, he was the one she loved.

They walked through the grass, hip brushing hip, thighs close, hearts tense, and soon, as if by tacit agreement, they reached the spot where they had first picnicked.

"In the universe," Dan said softly, putting his hands at her waist, "I'd say this was one of my favorite spots." His eyes softened. "For in this spot I knew how much I wanted you . . . and how much I loved being with you."

She smiled and wrapped her arms around him, and in the silence they gazed at each other, their eyes bright in the moonlight. He pulled her close, and moments later they were lying in the softness of the grass with their arms around each other but their bodies not quite touching. "I want to look into those eyes and see what I've been thinking about all week," he murmured. Tantalizingly he pulled her against him so she could feel the firmness of his thighs against her bare legs, the rise and fall of his chest against her own. "You never lie with your eyes, Marina. And all week I've been imagining those eyes saying yes, that you're ready."

"You're not the only one who's been imagining," she whispered. "I've imagined this very scene over and over—in thoughts, in dreams, with your eyes looking into mine as they are now, with your body even closer." At her words, he crossed his thigh over hers, half-covering her with his body.

"Like this?" he asked softly, smiling but with eyes deeply serious.

Her breath came faster. "Even closer," she whispered, and he put his warm hand around her waist, under her shirt, where her senses were awakened with warmth.

"And then what?" he whispered. "How much have you wanted me in your thoughts and in your dreams?"

Her eyes burned into his. "As much as you've wanted me," she murmured and put a hand against his rough cheek. She loved him so much—loved his clear, dark eyes, the feel of his skin, the warmth she felt with his every breath, every word, every touch. "Maybe I've wanted you even more," she whispered.

"Oh, Marina." He enveloped her tightly in his arms and covered her mouth with his, and they shared a kiss that seemed to say all that needed to be said, a kiss that was deep, loving, desperate.

He pulled away and brushed her dark hair back

125

from her eyes. "You've talked about your thoughts," he breathed, running a hand along her shorts to where her thigh was bare, searing it with his persuasive stroke. "You've talked about your dreams," he rasped, his fingers sending waves of hot need through her. "But I need to know about now, Marina." He roved his lips down along her throat.

"Oh, Dan," she murmured. "I want you."

She felt his body respond to her words with a tremor that was thrilling. "God, how I want that to be true," he whispered. "But Marina, you've said it before when you've needed me physically. I don't want you to be sorry . . . to regret . . . to think you acted too quickly."

As he spoke his hands conveyed the opposite of the caution he was voicing. For as he told her that perhaps they should wait, that perhaps she wasn't ready, he stroked her inner thigh with a heated urgency that drove all thoughts but desire from her mind. "Dan," she whispered, yearning for him with a liquid need that was like fire. Her hands found the buttons of his shirt and hurriedly undid them, and at that first sensation of skin against skin, her fingertips running through the hair covering his firmly muscled chest, she wanted him desperately.

As she pressed her lips to his and with a moan roved downward, he moved a warm, persuasive hand up along her thigh and under the edge of her shorts, and she cried out as she writhed in need of a deeper touch. Her lips found the hardness of one of his nipples, and as she took it in her mouth and then gently tugged it with her teeth, he moaned "Marina" in a voice that set her awash with desire.

His touch grew more urgent as he unfastened her shorts and parted the fabric with questing fingers. His hand was warm, strong, coaxing, and Marina was torn between the fiery wish that Dan would continue forever and the aching need to have him more fully, to feel the pulsating strength of his desire united with hers. "Dan," she whispered, her voice hoarse, her lips wet against his chest. "I need you. I want you."

With his hands he urged her upward until she was once again looking into his deep brown eyes. In their clear depths she was certain she saw love, and as he whispered "Darling," she was certain she heard it. His movements were gentle yet quick as he began to undress her. She watched him—his breath quickening as he parted her blouse, his eyes darkening in pleasure as he finally slipped off her shorts. "So beautiful," he whispered, and with warm, gentle hands pulled off her last remaining garment.

She warmed under his dark, appreciative gaze, and her pleasure grew in knowing she looked her best for him, her nipples hardened in desire, her breasts full, her skin flushed with the heat of passion.

"Come. Let me," she whispered, reaching out to unfasten his belt buckle. She wanted to linger and hurry at one and the same time, to draw out the pleasure of waiting as much as she could, but when her fingers found the muscled flesh beneath his belt she knew she could wait no more. As she pulled off each piece of clothing, exposing slim hips, long lean legs, the strong muscles of his chest, she grew closer and closer to a blazing ache, running her fingers along fine-haired skin she wanted rubbing against her own more than anything. His hands ran lightly over her hips and along her thighs, warming her silken skin to fiery desire, and she pulled off his last piece of clothing breathlessly. At the sight of his lean form, aroused and eager, she pulled him close, wanting to feel the heat of his damp skin, the strength of his muscles against her.

His eyes penetrated hers as for one timeless moment he held back—waiting, tantalizing her with his nearness—and then he was hers in a blazing, rapturous surge of love. He took her upward on a spiraling path of pleasure, urging her on with soft oaths of passion, moaning in rapture. "Marina," he rasped, "for so long I've wanted you."

"Oh Dan, yes," she moaned, and together they cried out in ecstasy as their love burst into shuddering release. Afterward they lay in each other's arms, smooth cheek against rough one, breathing slow and satisfied, hearts still beating as one.

Dan reached up and brushed a strand of wet hair from Marina's forehead and shifted so he could look into her eyes. "You're so beautiful," he said softly, gazing at her. "And so wonderful." He smiled. "I knew the time was right. Making love takes care of so many things." He put a hand on the curve of her hip and pulled her closer. His touch felt possessive in the nicest of ways, and Marina knew he was right that lovemaking smoothed out many problems. For she was more filled with love for him than ever before: she loved him, she belonged with him, she knew they were meant for each other in the deepest of ways. And wasn't that more important than anything else?

"I care so much for you," he murmured, and then he frowned, his dark brows knitting in concern. "I feel so right about you, about us." He sighed. "But let's not question anything. Let's take each day as it comes, all right? As we did tonight."

She looked into his deep brown eyes, fringed with dark lashes, edged with small laugh lines at the outer corners. She loved them so much; she loved him so much; and she didn't want to say anything to disturb the waters. He leaned forward and kissed her softly, lovingly, on the lips. "I've felt this way from the beginning," he said. "Wanting to be with you, finding reasons against it, and then in the end doing what felt so right one could never question it. But I found something interesting, Marina. Something I brought you that seems so . . . relevant."

She looked at him questioningly. "What?"

"Tatiana's memoirs," he said. "What she left for you in the will."

Marina frowned. "You read them?"

Dan had an odd look in his eyes. "Strangely enough," he said, "she wanted me to read them. She mentioned it several times, and always with that inimitable gleam in her eye."

"I wonder why," Marina mused.

He smiled. "You've got to see it," he said, hefting himself up to a sitting position. "I'll get it for you."

Almost involuntarily she reached out, not wanting to be separated so soon.

He took her hand and squeezed it, then held it and brushed it against his cheek and across his lips. "I'll be right back." As he turned and walked toward the inn, Marina watched, astonished at the power that was deep within those lean muscles, the strength and rhythm that could please so fully and deeply. And she realized that even something as insignificant as watching him walk across the grass now caused an almost physical feeling of loss. She belonged with him.

When he came back to sit beside her, she smiled and snuggled up against him, and together they opened the book. In the light flooding from the inn, Marina could see that the first several pages were photographs taped onto the old gray paper of the album. Dated eighty and more years before, they were snapshots and some formal portraits of Tatiana as a small child and the rest of the family as they were getting ready to leave Russia for the long trip to America. Everyone had a different expression—one looked happy but apprehensive, another as if he was ready to take on the world. And Tatiana, a little girl in a lavishly embroidered dress, looked thoughtful and serious, but with a spark of mischief as bright as the moon in her large brown eyes. Underneath the picture it said, "I was scared but knew it would all be fun if I made it so."

Marina smiled. "I haven't seen these in years."

Dan smiled, too. "Well, we can look at these later. But I really want to show you the part I was talking about, Marina—the 1917 part—it's eerie." He turned past several pages of pictures, most labeled with long descriptions but others with merely a question mark or, sometimes, an exclamation point. And then he stopped when he came to a series of photographs on beige paper that had been bound together and then slipped into the album. There was much more writing than in the rest of the album. The pictures were of a young Tatiana, perhaps twenty-three or twenty-four—dark-eyed, beautiful, in a summer dress that showed off a figure that was voluptuous but not heavy. Marina recognized the setting as Windy Hill years and years ago, on the lawn with the inn in the background. Tatiana was smiling, with laughter in her eyes and flowers in her hair.

And with her was a man Marina had never seen: young, though older than Tatiana, dark-eyed and dark-haired, handsome in a surprising way. His nose was not quite right, somehow, for his face, yet the irregularity was magnetic, more attractive than one would ever expect. His hair was long, jet black, luxurious, and probably somewhat avant-garde for the time, and his cheekbones were high, like Tatiana's and Marina's. His arm was around the young Tatiana's waist, and he was laughing, facing the camera but looking sidelong at Tatiana. And though he was laughing, perhaps in response to something the unknown photographer had said, it was his eyes that were most compelling. For in them as they looked at Tatiana one could see love, joy, a secret they didn't need or want to share with anyone else.

"It was a secret, wasn't it?" Marina asked softly.

Dan nodded, and she looked again at the photograph—so filled with happiness, yet tinged as well with sadness.

"You can just tell," she said. "By the looks in their eyes." She looked at Dan. "Who was he?" she asked.

He nodded at the album. "Read what Tatiana wrote under the photographs." He sighed. "She says it all better than I ever could."

Marina turned to the album and began to read:

"Me and Andrei, laughing at nothing. At that moment I knew how much I loved him. I could feel he loved me more—even though I felt as if all the love in the world were bursting from my heart. When I saw his eyes, I knew. And I knew also that tragedy would come someday to the two of us. That, too, I knew from his eyes."

The next picture was of Andrei building a stone wall, one that was still on the grounds, near the creek. "Our dear good friend was no longer here to take the photos," Tatiana had written. "Never again were we pictured together, the way we loved life more than any other. But I loved this picture too because it showed Andrei's great strength and his love for work and the outdoors. Look into his eyes and you can see it."

The next several pictures were of, alternately, Andrei and Tatiana working on the house—painting, cutting grass, planting, sawing wood—and there was a running commentary underneath: "I knew nothing then, only that I wanted to own this wonderful house, and that I needed someone to help me. I had saved every penny, sewn more dresses for more Park

132

Avenue ladies than all my friends together. And I had done something nobody had thought I could do. But then I was alone, with not enough money to finish the work, no one to tell me I was not crazy to think I could do what I wanted. In those days, Marina—" Marina stopped reading and looked at Dan. "She wrote this for me?"

He smiled and nodded. "When you started college," he said. "She loved doing it."

Marina smiled and read on. "In those days, Marina, a woman did not go off by herself the way I did. But I knew what I wanted more than anyone else, and I did what I wanted no matter what anyone thought. My family was not speaking with me because I had fled an arranged marriage. And I was alone in a world I hardly knew. I did not know what had happened to the man I was supposed to marry, a weak accountant from Lvov. And I did not care. I knew I would make a terrible wife for him—I disliked everything about him and could never have loved him. And I cared nothing for what anyone else thought. And then, when I needed some stonework done, a man in town told me someone named Andrei Komikarroff was the best; he had just arrived from Kiev and lived with his two brothers in the next town. He spoke almost no English, but he was the finest stonecutter there was. My heart leaped when I heard his name—someone I could talk Russian with!

"Well, my dearest granddaughter, we fell in love, but it was a love filled with pain. From the first day I knew of Andrei's life in Russia. Naturally we spoke

133

for hours of our homeland. And I knew from the start that he was a married man with a beautiful five-year-old boy. He had fought for the revolution, a cause I believed in with him, but then the revolutionaries had turned against him, and he had fled in danger. He had left quickly, leaving behind his wife and son to come later, as soon as he could send the money. But after he had gone, his wife, Sonya, had become as involved in the fight as he had been, and now she was in great peril, unable to leave, in danger every moment she stayed.

"I respected her greatly. I felt then that my plans for my own life were shallow and without meaning. Andrei and I talked much of politics, of the revolution and our roles. And I could see he was torn between the love we had created and his deep commitment to his country.

"In the magical atmosphere of Windy Hill, Marina, we fell in love. We worked sometimes twenty hours a day, and we made our love fill the past, the present, and the future with its light. But always it was as if we both had knives in our chests. We hated ourselves for what we were doing and for what we had done. We said to each other, 'We were brought together for a reason. Love like this could not come along by chance.' But we couldn't find any answers. I lived for his dark brown eyes, Marina, for his laugh that made me cry because I knew I would not hear it much longer, and for the strength of his arms.

"He looked always tortured. He wept. He loved me more than anything, anyone in the world. But he could never leave his wife and son, fighting back home, in danger at every moment. He knew he would go back. When he had money for passage and word that the time was relatively safe, he would go.

"I should have known when he finished the stone wall that he would leave. For three days afterward he came to me and we finished much of the other work we had begun together—the work that had brought us together so that we could fall in love. But his eyes were in pain when he looked at me, and I should have known the time had arrived.

"The first morning of July I woke up and knew he would not come to me. I wept, hoping he would come to brush away the tears, and we would hold each other and know we had more time. But he never came.

"I visited his two brothers the next day. Andrei was gone, they said. They knew nothing of me except that I was the woman Andrei had been working for. I held back my tears and left.

"Andrei wrote to me only once after that. He would always love me, he said. I knew it was true, but I knew also that what I loved about him—his commitment to what he believed in and his fierce, fiery integrity—were what would keep him from me always.

"You know, Marina, that I eventually opened Windy Hill and lived there for many years. When I decided to sell it, the decision was very painful—my first great love had been born in that beautiful, enchanted place. And now, by the time you read this, Windy Hill will have been turned into something else.

135

"Marina, if you are wondering whether the grandfather you never met is the man I was supposed to marry, the one I called the weakling, the answer is no. (If you did, shame! What sort of woman do you think your Tatiana was?) I would never have given in to my family. For what?

"But Marina, the truth is that I did not love your grandfather Vassily the way I had loved Andrei. Vassily, too, was Russian. He, too, helped me with Windy Hill, on the landscaping and the heavy work I was unable to do. Once again I felt myself falling in love—with Vassily's enjoyment of the warm sun on his back as he worked, with his beautiful eyes, blue but as deep as Andrei's, with so much that was so similar to Andrei.

"We married. I made up with my family, who had not meant for me to be unhappy but only married. Who I married, as long as he was not a crook, did not matter.

"But I realized too late, Marina, that what I loved about Vassily was Andrei, and the idea of love, which had made my life so happy and so sad.

"It was saddest for Vassily. He knew. He knew of my feelings before I did. He was in love with me and didn't care.

"I grew to love him for himself, Marina. But it took many, many years, and he was a wonderful man I had to discover without the past and the memory of Andrei interfering.

"Marina, after Vassily died I was so sad; sadder than I ever felt about Andrei. I had loved Vassily so much, and I had been unfair to him. He was strong and wonderful and smart and handsome, and he had loved me as much as anyone can hope for.

"I miss him so much, and I miss the days when I was angry at him for being different than I had thought, for not being Andrei; I would like to live them over and love him as he deserved to be loved.

"I had thought of Andrei as my great great love, but he was like a dream. We were meant to be together only for a short time. Maybe to point us each on our path.

"My granddaughter, I've always interfered in your life, and I see no reason to stop now. You are in college. You are beautiful, as I always knew you would be, and stubborn, as I had always hoped.

"Two things I want to convey to you, which I couldn't have without telling you about the beginnings of Windy Hill, and Vassily and Andrei. Remember, no one in the family knows of Andrei—not because I ever cared what they thought, but because Andrei would not have wanted anyone to know. It is many years past, and you are meant to know of it now. But I want you to learn from what I did, so you gain what good I received and avoid the pain I created for myself.

"You will have many men, I am sure, who will fall in love with you. Look at the picture at the top of this page, at your grandfather Vassily in love with me completely. And look at me, forcing a smile. I was in the period when I had discovered Vassily was not the man I had thought. I was a fool, Marina, but it can happen to anyone who has a great desire to love and be loved—to make the man into someone he's

137

not so you can love him. And then you are trapped. I was lucky, but usually one is not.

"You come from a family filled with love. You and Alex fight like cats and dogs, but underneath there is love, and there is great love between your parents. You are going to be very hungry for that same kind of love. But let it happen without force, without intention, without design. And you will be happy forever.

"And maybe you can find a place like Windy Hill, someplace that is so beautiful it almost creates love. If you find it, do not let it go. And be happy, my dear Marina, forever and ever."

Marina sighed and closed the book, its torn leather cover with Tatiana's unmistakable script saying: "Tatiana's Photos and Memorys" crossed out and made "Memories."

Marina turned to Dan and looked into his beautiful brown eyes, wondering if she felt now as Tatiana had with Andrei . . . or Vassily, in the end. "It's strange," she said quietly. "And here we are at Windy Hill."

He smiled. "Reliving the past, in a sense." He paused. "And Marina, she wanted to be sure I read it, too."

They looked into each other's eyes and said nothing.

CHAPTER SEVEN

Dan arranged to take the next week off from work. The principals in the main case he was working on were making a major decision that would concern him only later on, and he spent the next seven days with Marina.

The week was idyllic. They worked in the mornings, made love in the afternoons, talked and laughed and made love at night. They lived in a way Marina loved—physically, close to the earth, in the clean fresh air and sun, with the smells of the sun and the earth and the wildflowers in their hair, and the sky and the light of the moon reflected in their eyes at night. They made love by the brook, in the wildflowers, in the moonlight under the stars.

Dan seemed to know everything—the calls of the animals at night and the birds at dawn, the names of plants and fish and trees, the best ways to catch and clean and cook the trout they caught, the most beautiful spots for making love. On the ridge beyond the creek they picnicked and looked out at the rest of the mountain range, and Dan pointed out rocks he had climbed and areas that were particularly dangerous. He was filled with the woods and the sun and the earth, filled with knowledge that had been buried for too long, and each time Marina saw this she fell more deeply in love.

On Sunday afternoon, as they lay in the warm sun along the sandy edge of the creek, Marina looked at Dan and smiled. "You look so much more relaxed than when I saw you in the city at the reading of the will. The country really does you good."

He leaned forward and kissed her lightly on the mouth. "The country and you, Marina." He turned over and lay on his back, looking up at the sky. "I'd like to spend more time here, but I'm going to have to get back tonight." He turned his head to her. "And you should, too. We've been lazy this week, and—"

"Lazy!" she cried, smiling. "I'm exhausted!"

"But, ah, is it all from work?" he asked. "Face it—we took an incredibly pleasurable but indulgent break by working half-days this week. If you really want to do this, Marina, you've got to do what your grandmother did—work twenty-hour days."

Marina was tempted to add, With the man she loved, but kept silent instead. "Then why should I go to the city?" she asked. "I have a million things to do up here."

"That's true," he said. "But amazing as this may

140

sound, Marina, you're really just about ready to start decorating and things like that. And you said you wanted to get whatever it is you need—fabrics, I guess—from some store on Madison Avenue."

"Mmm. Laura Ashley," she said. "They have beautiful fabrics—all with tiny prints and muted colors that would make the inn look great."

He smiled and stretched and laced his hands behind his head. "The inn," he said, sounding pleased. "We've actually almost done it. Now if I can get away this week before Friday, I'll be up. Otherwise, this weekend. And the permits should be ready this week, in any case. But I'll be back." He grinned. "The irresistible attractions of Marina Tolchin and Windy Hill are both turning my professional life upside down, but I'm happy."

Marina leaned up on one elbow, leaned over, and kissed him on the mouth. He pulled her on top of him and looked into her eyes. "Every time you kiss me," he murmured, "it's more exciting than the last time . . . and I can't believe that anyone's lips could be so moist and soft, anyone's mouth so sweet." He ran his hands through her hair. "I'll never get enough of you," he whispered. "So easy to make love to, so fantastic to please."

"Oh, Dan," she murmured, her voice hoarse. "Make love to me."

He gazed into her eyes with blazing passion. "You don't have to say any more," he said huskily, enveloping her in his strong arms.

Their skins were warm from the sun, lubricious from the suntan lotion. Dan pulled Marina's bikini top off with urgent fingers; his eyes were fiery with pleasure as he gazed at her full breasts and rolled her over so she was looking up at him. As he lowered his head and covered a breast with his warm, wet lips, he parted her legs with his and then clasped a leg with his hard thighs, holding her in a grip that was as fierce as his lips were gentle. With wet lips and teasing bites he brought each nipple to a hardened excitement that sent warm liquid through Marina's whole body, and then he moved his mouth downward, over the smooth skin of her stomach to the edge of her bikini. Tantalizingly his fingers worked along the bottom edge as his mouth worked along the top, and Marina began to writhe in need beneath his coaxing fingers and tongue as they edged away the fabric and hungrily fed her desire. She pulled at his hair, moaned his name, cried out as she was engulfed with blazing need.

"Dan," she moaned.

He looked at her with stormy dark eyes, and his fingers grasped her bikini. "I don't think we need this anymore," he said hoarsely and pulled it down and off. His hands found her once again and at one touch set her to a flaming pitch. "Dan," she cried, and reached for him. She ran her fingers over the fabric of his bathing suit, and the strength of his desire trembled under her touch.

"Marina," he whispered hoarsely, and with quick tugging movements she pulled his suit off. He moved on top of her then, enveloping her in strength and warmth and love, and then with a blazing thrust, they were together at last. They melted into each other and grasped, coaxed, writhed with desire, cried out in pleasure. Their love was quick and deep under the sun, following a rhythm that came from the heat, from desire that had grown all morning, from new knowledge of how to please and be pleased. And when their passion exploded in coursing ecstasy, the pleasure seemed greater than ever before. It was only moments later, when thought returned, that they could know they felt as they always did afterward: that their lovemaking had never been better.

She lay with her head on his chest, he with his warm hands around her back. Together they listened to the sounds of the creek and the birds, sounds that had been drowned out by sounds of love minutes earlier. And Marina wondered if Dan was as happy as she was.

He left that night, promising her he'd be back as soon as he could get away from his office, and promising with his eyes that he wished he were staying.

After he was gone, Marina thought about Tatiana's story. When Tatiana had seen Andrei for the last time, she hadn't even known for sure that it was the end; she had suspected, but he had never told her. Marina knew her own situation was vastly different in every way, but she wondered nonetheless: How long would Dan continue coming and going, living two separate and distinct existences? He seemed incomparably happier at Windy Hill; but most of the times the thought occurred to her, she didn't even broach the subject. For as it was she was surprised and pleased that Dan was throwing himself into the project and her life as enthusiastically as he was.

But she couldn't help drawing negative comparisons between her own situation and that of Tatiana, when Tatiana had tried to make her husband into something he wasn't. Marina was already fantasizing about Dan quitting his job and opening an office in town, leaving the city altogether and being with her. Was she being completely unrealistic? She felt as if Dan was rediscovering his priorities and desires for the first time in years, and that she was his encouragement and, in a sense, method of doing so; but perhaps she was wrong.

Marina stayed on at Windy Hill for a few days after Dan left, building shelves in the kitchen and taking measurements for curtains, wallpaper, and rugs. She hurriedly planted a small herb garden—essential for her cooking—right outside the back door to the kitchen, and then she returned to New York City for the first time in weeks.

She went shopping—a horrible, crowded, seemingly interminable experience compared to the shopping she had done upstate—and then returned to her apartment. She wanted to call Dan to let him know she was in town, but she felt strangely reluctant to do so. For the last time she had seen Dan in the city—admittedly much earlier in their relationship—she had been much, much less fond of him than she was now.

But when she called him, as soon as she heard the

enthusiasm in his voice, the obvious affection and pleasure, she wondered why she had even hesitated.

Dan arrived at her apartment at eleven that evening, after working late and eating at the office. He looked exhausted—haggard, even—and his rumpled suit looked as if he had slept in it. He took her in his arms and kissed her—long, hard, with an urgency and need that shocked her—and then tore his mouth away. "God, that feels great," he said. "*You* feel great. In my arms. The only face I've been glad to see today. And definitely the only one I've wanted to kiss."

Marina smiled and ran her fingers through his hair. "Well, I'm glad to hear *that,* but you look exhausted, darling."

He grinned and tilted his head. " 'Darling.' I think I like the sound of that. That's the first time you've ever called me that." He paused and winked. "At least while we're not making love." He covered her lips with his, drawing her against a body already fully aroused. "Darling," he grated into her ear. "God, how I've missed you."

With his desire so evident, his breath so hot in her ear, his voice so hoarse with male need, she was swamped with desire, arching her body against his, molding herself to him in desperate wanting. "Come," she whispered. "I want you."

"Oh, Marina," he whispered, and kissed her deeply before leading her into the bedroom and onto the bed. His touch was feverish as he took her clothes off, her touch tantalizing as she began to undress him. She lingered where she knew it would arouse him most, playing with his nipples, running her hands along his thighs and teasingly passing over the fastening of his pants. She meant to entice, to draw out the anticipation as much as she could, but when he reached for her and cupped her breasts in his warm hands, she moaned with pleasure and leaned down to cover his lips with her own.

He pulled her on top of him, wrapping his strong, warm arms around her and then running them along her back, over her hips, across the silk of her thighs in strokes that grew increasingly urgent. She drew her head back and looked into his eyes with a smile. "Remember the days when we had to hold back?"

Her breath caught as he moved his fingers upward along her thighs. "I don't know how we ever did it," she murmured huskily, struggling to find her voice through thickened waves of desire.

His eyes were heavy with need. "I don't know how we're doing it now," he whispered hoarsely.

He pulled her to him once more and drew her into a deep kiss. Awakened with deeper need, she eased away, trailing her lips downward; his warm hands guided her until her lips found the line of fine dark hair going into his waistband, and her fingers found the fastening of his pants. Slowly she removed the last of his clothing, all the while planting gentle kisses and playful bites that made him whisper her name with an urgency that was like a deeply pleasurable caress.

"Marina, come," he whispered, pulling her upward so she was looking down into his eyes. And with firmly guiding hands he brought her onto him

146

in a deep surge of pleasure, then into a rhythm that was slow and rolling, coursing into a blazing frenzy and deep, rapturous release.

Gently their bodies relaxed—damp, satisfied, spent. Marina lay on top of Dan, enjoying the feel of his breath against her cheek, but then an unexpected sadness crept into her heart. She felt uneasy, as if there was something wrong, and as she rolled over on to her back, she knew what was bothering her. She wanted to be back in the country. She looked up at the ceiling—so plain, so blank, so different from looking up at sky, moon, stars, or even being indoors but hearing the sounds of nighttime in the mountains.

"I don't see how I managed to grow up here," she said quietly. "You'd think that since I was born here and spent so much of my life here, I would be used to it. And I always was. But now I feel like a caged animal in this apartment—with people above me, below me, to either side of me."

He turned on his side and put a warm hand across her stomach. "That's because so far you've had a wonderful time up there. The weather's been beautiful, everything has gone your way, we've had some incredible times. But that's the best, Marina. It won't always be like that."

She turned to look at him. "That's not what you used to say about country living," she said.

"That was a long time ago." He reached over and grasped her shoulder. "Come here," he said, and she shifted so she was facing him. "You remember what Tatiana wrote?" he asked softly. "She wrote about something that has a lot to do with us. She wanted you never to try to make someone what he's not."

Marina frowned. "Don't use something my grandmother wrote—and to me, Dan, not to you—just to try to prove a point."

"I'm not 'using' it, Marina, any more than she would have wanted. If you remember, she wanted me to read it, too."

Marina looked away. "That was just some legal thing," she said.

He touched her chin and turned her to face him again. "You know it wasn't," he said quietly, gazing into her eyes. "She liked me—and she used to show me all kinds of things she had written. My appointments with her always lasted half a day," he said with a laugh.

She winked. "And I'll bet you charged her for half an hour."

He shrugged. "She was my favorite client. Why not?"

Marina smiled, but moments later her smile faded. "What you said before—about my trying to make you into something you're not. What makes you so sure of everything whenever we're talking about us or our relationship?"

Dan shook his head. "I'm not sure of anything. Not anymore. But I know your enthusiasms, Marina. You've always thrown yourself into whatever interests you had at the moment. And I don't want you to think I'm something I'm not. To misinterpret."

She looked at him skeptically. "If you're worried

that I think you're the Marlboro man ready to jump onto his horse and ride off into the sunset, forget it." She sat up and swung her legs over the side of the bed. "Why don't you go back to your nice Wall Street office and get back to work," she said quietly. "I thought we were sharing something really nice. I had no idea I was forcing you into a major personality change."

"Marina." He reached out and found her hand, but she shook loose and stood up. She turned and looked at him, now sitting up in the bed; it was difficult not to think of their recent lovemaking as she looked at him, but then her anger returned more strongly than before.

"I mean it," she said, her voice thick with wrath. "It doesn't feel very good to think you're operating on a totally different level from someone else." She raised her chin. "And I'd rather be alone for a while if you don't mind. Or even if you do."

He stood up and came around to where she stood with her arms crossed. He grasped her wrists, but she whipped around and stalked away. "I mean it," she repeated. "I just . . . I have to think about all this. And I have to do it alone."

He came around behind her and encircled her in his arms, resting his chin on top of her head. "Marina," he said quietly. "Don't," he murmured. "We don't really have a problem. You're creating one because we're growing so close . . . closer, perhaps, than you had planned."

She turned to face him. "Uh-uh," she said. "That's the way you feel. Remember you're the one who

149

plans—plans to have a casual relationship; plans not to fall in love; plans to keep everything simple."

His eyes softened. "Planning doesn't always work," he said quietly. "No matter how much you think it will." He put his arms around her and drew her against him, holding her head gently against his chest. The soft-scratchy feel of it brought forth memories of their lovemaking, its warmth, the heat of their passion, and she felt tears begin to well up as she held her cheek against his skin.

"Oh Dan, I love you so much," she said quietly, her voice closing over rising tears. "I just wish things were as uncomplicated as they used to be."

Tenderly he tilted her chin up and looked into her eyes. "It was always complicated . . . always deep between us." He paused. "It always will be. Marina, every time I leave you it hurts me. It's difficult every time I come back to the city and think of the pleasures we've shared . . . the pleasure of just being with you . . . and they're pleasures I'm keeping from myself." He frowned. "But I think it's right that we're apart—that we can each do what we're meant to do. I'm meant to work here in the city, and you're meant to be up there at Windy Hill right now. Neither one of us would be happy if it were any different. But let's realize what our differences are. We're both at points in our lives where we're changing. And the only way we can discover if we really know each other is if we're together *and* apart, living as we're meant to live, discovering what that means in each of us." He sighed. "I just keep thinking you still think I'm the man you knew in college. And if that's true, it just can't work."

She said nothing. When she looked into his eyes, all she could think of was the fact that she had just told him she loved him, and his only response was to talk a blue streak. But he obviously believed what he was saying: he believed she didn't really know him, he believed they should pursue their careers separately, and there was nothing, really, that she could do to change the way he felt.

"I guess then that I'll see you up there," she said quietly. She could have said much more: that she wouldn't be able to go on with the relationship much longer as it stood now, that as each day dawned she felt more and more certain that she couldn't live with what they had and couldn't live without it. But she said nothing; for she believed—indeed, had to believe —that his feelings were shifting, that as each day passed he wanted to be with her more and more. And these were feelings that clearly could not be forced or pushed or strengthened by anything she said.

But as she looked into his eyes and gently broke away from him to get dressed once more—to feel a separation that was more difficult each time it occurred—she wondered whether he'd ever really change.

The next day Marina returned to Windy Hill with more clothes and all the fabric she had bought. She had found exactly what she wanted—a tiny red-and-white print for the commons room, blue and beige for the dining room, and Provençale for the other rooms—but she wasn't even looking forward to putting them up. For she was consumed once again with doubts about Windy Hill, doubts she knew were her way of avoiding thinking about Dan.

But soon after she arrived she was confronted with another set of problems. Her brother Alex called, having just returned from a business trip to the Virgin Islands, and he was furious. He had just spoken to Dan and found that "even the damn lawyer for the estate," as he put it, was in favor of what Marina was doing. And so he was coming up the next morning to see exactly what she had done.

Marina was both annoyed and annoyingly nervous: what, after all, did she really care what her brother thought about what she was doing? Why couldn't she be like Tatiana, who had forsaken her family rather than do something she dreaded in order to please them? Of course, in a sense she *was* acting independently, having made plans to open Windy Hill despite Alex's objections. But she realized this didn't make her truly happy, either. For what she wanted was to work *with* Alex, to have him be as enthusiastic and hopeful as she that it would work. And since it was what Tatiana had wished for, she would try her best to make it happen.

But when he got to Windy Hill Alex was more negative than ever. When he first arrived, Marina had seen the surprise in his eyes and had known he was impressed with how much she had accomplished, for she knew that Alex and Dan had discussed the inn's condition. But Alex had hidden his approval thoroughly and was now slumped in one of the antique couches Marina had bought, holding forth on what a mistake she had made.

"Why don't you leave?" Marina suddenly interrupted. "I didn't ask you to come, you know."

He blinked, caught off guard by her bluntness, and he looked so hurt that Marina had to hold herself back from going to comfort him. "I'm sorry," she said. "I don't really mean that. But I just don't feel like listening to criticism that I don't think you even believe yourself. Alex, I'd like you to work on the inn with me—not to live here, but to participate. Why don't you give it a try?"

He looked at her, his uncertain blue eyes mirrors of her own. For a moment she thought he was going to say yes, that he'd try, at least, to help make the inn work. But he opened his mouth, closed it, and then sighed. "Why don't you just leave me alone?" he finally said, his voice hollow. "You haven't once considered my feelings in all this, Marina. You haven't once given me time to think. You've just gone ahead as quickly as you possibly could have, and I've been left with a big dose of guilt and nothing else."

"I asked you at the beginning," she said. "You were so definitely against it—"

"But I didn't know you were actually going to do it, Marina. You never give anybody a chance to come in on anything because you push so damn hard no one wants to. And you have to have everything your own way. All this old-fashioned crap"—he gestured around the commons room—"how do you know this was the best way to do it?"

"I don't know for a fact, Alex, but I've done this

whole project the way I've wanted, from start to finish. And I think it looks great." She paused. "Anyway, you can hardly expect me to decorate the place like Howard Johnson's. That would just be crazy."

"Maybe. But maybe not. Your problem, Marina, is that you're not living in the modern world. You think everything has to be perfect and old-fashioned —whether it's Windy Hill or a dinner or a relationship." He looked at her in challenge. "And you don't see how annoying that is to everyone else. This place is just sickeningly quaint."

She stood up and crossed her arms. "If that's the way you feel, you might as well leave now," she said as calmly as she could. "Good-bye." And she turned and walked out through the kitchen to the garden, where she began furiously weeding and trying to put Alex's words out of her mind. A few minutes later she heard the roar of his motor. She heard the crunch of gravel as his car pulled down the driveway, and then there was only the sound of the birds.

Over the next several days Marina managed to furnish the entire first floor with antique oak and walnut furniture she had bought at a local auction, along with a few maple Shaker pieces she found in an antique shop. She turned most of the former family living quarters on the first floor into guest rooms, leaving herself the bedroom closest to the kitchen. And soon, just as the herbs were beginning to grow and the summer was reaching its peak, she realized she was actually ready to open Windy Hill, to test the plans she had been, in a sense, hiding behind up until then. She had tested the kitchen over and over again, had found all the best markets in the area and made contacts with the local vegetable farmers, and she had done everything that had to be done except advertise. She set an opening date, planned the ads she'd put in local papers and New York City magazines, and called Dan to give him the news.

But his secretary said he had been called away to an emergency consultation with clients in Texas and that she could only give Dan a message to call Marina. Marina was surprised that Dan was in Texas already; he had told her about the case, a products-liability one in which a young boy's family was suing Dan's client, the manufacturer of a toy that had exploded. Dan and Marina hadn't talked much about it—it was Dan's most time-consuming and least favorite case—but from what Dan had told her, she had thought the company was simply going to settle and that the case would never see the inside of a courtroom.

When Dan called her that night, he sounded tired and disheartened. "You sound terrible," Marina said. "What happened?"

"A complete turnaround," he said. "My client doesn't want to settle anymore. They're actually considering letting the case go to trial."

"What have you advised them?" she asked.

"Well, settlement means less money for the firm. But if the case goes to trial, the client has a good chance of losing, since these days liability doesn't depend on actual negligence as much as it used to— thank God. But I'm in a bind, Marina. Settlement is

155

the only smart course and the only just course, because although the amount will be less than what a jury would award, the kid's family won't have to wait ten years to get the money. Cases like this sometimes take more than ten years to get through all the pretrial maneuevers. But damnit, the company doesn't want to pay." He sighed. "Well. Enough of that for now—what about you? How's the inn going?" He paused. "I miss you like hell already, and I'm probably going to be out here for weeks."

"Oh, no! I was calling to tell you—I'm going to open the inn."

"When?"

"Well, I was thinking this Friday. Anything beyond then is really putting it off, and if I'm going to get any summer business, I have to start now."

"Damn," he said quietly. There was a silence. Then he said, "Can't you wait a bit? I'd like to be there with you to open it."

She sighed. "I'd like that, too," she said. "But how long are you going to be out there? I can't wait too long."

"That's the problem," he said. "Could be another day, could be another month."

"Then I can't," she answered. "I can't lose that much time."

"Damn. We worked so hard," he said. "Well, look. I can't argue, because I know you're right— you need every day to build up your clientele, especially since you'll be essentially a weekend business at the beginning. But listen—do me a favor, darling."

She smiled. "What's that?"

"Call me after your first evening. We'll drink champagne together over the phone—you at the inn and me in my sad little hotel room. It isn't the kind of celebration I'd usually have in mind, but it's better than nothing."

"Mm," she said. "But I hope you're back by then, anyway."

"Darling, if I'm back by then, our celebration will be anything but long-distance; close, intimate, incredibly deep would be more what I had in mind."

"Sounds good to me," she said, smiling. "And wish me luck."

"You know I do, darling," he said softly. "Goodbye."

It was only after she hung up that Marina realized how truly disappointed she was that Dan wouldn't be able to be with her at the inn's opening. For it made her feel as if all the weeks of preparation, the weeks of happiness and lovemaking, had been a mere interlude, a wonderful and exciting time that was over forever, a prelude to an end rather than a beginning. Once again she thought of Tatiana's story; then, too, there had been the promise of something new—Windy Hill—and excitement over a beginning; and then, with a warning that was ignored, an abrupt end. Something in Dan's tone of voice had hinted that he had perhaps thought of all the work on the inn as an interesting escape from the "real" world; it was now time to get back to work, and if he could visit, that would be wonderful—but it would be a visit only, another break from reality to be celebrated in a pleasurable but transitory way.

But then Marina remembered that at the beginning, when she had first planned to open Windy Hill, she had intended on doing it alone, with no thoughts of men except that she wanted to escape from the ones she knew. And though much had happened since then, she knew she was perfectly capable of carrying through her plans.

And so that afternoon she placed her first ads in the local papers, announcing the opening of Windy Hill—French *cuisine minceur* and country lodgings. And she readied herself for one of the biggest gambles of her life.

CHAPTER EIGHT

The night of the inn's opening Marina was as nervous as if she had never cooked a meal in her entire life. She had hired two people to help her—two young women from town who would help out in the kitchen and as waitresses—but her biggest fear was that no one would show up at all. At the last minute, as she surveyed the dining room—lovely at last with its pale patterned linen tablecloths, beautiful curtains, and sprays of wildflowers and dried herbs—she realized she should have called some friends from the city just so she'd have *some* customers. But lately she had been so busy she had fallen out of touch with virtually everyone but Dan, and now, she supposed, she was paying the price.

But at six o'clock, as Marina and her two helpers nervously sipped wine in the kitchen and pretended nothing was amiss, the first customers—a young couple new to the area—arrived; and within an hour three more groups had come.

The evening flew by. Even with just ten customers there was a tremendous amount of work, for Marina had carelessly made the menu too extensive and almost everyone ordered something different. But the hard work made the time go quickly, and at the end of the evening, after receiving what seemed like very sincere compliments and fervent wishes of good luck from all the customers, Marina and her helpers collapsed around the kitchen table and consumed more wine and lots and lots of leftovers.

At about midnight, too drunk to drink any champagne but with a glass of the red wine she had been drinking all night, Marina called Dan from her bedroom. She couldn't wait to tell him about the evening. But he wasn't in; he had checked out that day. And when she tried his New York apartment, he wasn't there, either. Pleased that he was probably on his way back to the city and happy that the night had gone so well, Marina settled into bed and fell into an exhausted sleep.

The next morning Marina left a message at Dan's office, but there was no word from him all day. Unconcerned—he was, after all, as busy as she—Marina spent the day working out the menu more carefully and teaching her assistants as much as she could about what she was doing. They received a few calls for dinner reservations—the most exciting events of the afternoon—and by the middle of the evening there were even more customers than there had been on Friday night. Some had heard about Windy Hill from friends who had come the night before, others had seen the ads, and others were friends of Judy and Lexie, Marina's two helpers. The dining room had a capacity of only sixty people, and Marina was realizing with amazement that the room was about half-full, when Dan walked in with a young couple who had been there the night before.

Dan looked wonderful—relaxed, happy, dressed as Marina loved to see him in a casual striped polo shirt and corduroy pants. He strode across the dining room and took Marina in his arms and kissed her softly as he held her close against him. When he drew his head back, there was a gleam in his dark eyes as he said, "I don't give a damn that everyone in the room is looking at us. I'm glad, because I've been wanting to kiss you like this for days; and I want everyone to know it." He smiled. "Marina, I'm so happy for you. The place looks fantastic."

She smiled. "I know. I can't believe how well we're doing. It hasn't hurt at all that Judy and Lexie have told the whole town their jobs here depend on our having good business, but I think the ad helped, too."

"How would you feel about a rave review in one of the most influential magazines on the East Coast?"

Marina laughed. "I think that might help," she said.

"Well, you've got it," he said. "You see the couple I came in with?"

She nodded. "They were here last night."

"Right. And they loved it. She's Margo Fenning of *East Side Living*—"

"The one Ellie knows, too?"

Dan nodded. "I had told them about you and asked them not to come opening night. But Margo had thought it was the only night they could make it for quite a while, and they came without me. Anyway, they were more than delighted to come back tonight with me, and the review is already on its way to the magazine."

Marina's face lit up. "Really? That's fantastic." She paused. "It didn't have anything to do with you, though, did it? I mean, I appreciate your help, but I wouldn't want—"

"Not at all," he said. "Except in terms of the speed with which she came up here. But absolutely not, Marina. Anyway, 'fantastic' will be an understatement when you read the review—I'll show it to you later. But let me introduce you. Can you sit down with us for a while?"

She smiled. "Well, it *is* my restaurant. Why not?"

Marina enjoyed the break and the company enormously. Margo Fenning and her husband Charles were charming and full of what seemed like endless praise for Marina's cooking; and though Marina had initially felt that there were certainly more interesting topics of discussion than the inn, Margo apparently wanted to talk of nothing else. She gave Marina dozens of bits of arcane information she had gleaned from other restaurateurs, and her confidence in the future success of Windy Hill made Marina very, very happy.

Occasionally, as Margo went on, Marina felt Dan's gaze upon her. And when she looked up, his eyes were full of desire, and full of humor as well, as if to say, This is all very nice but when are we going to be alone together?

Finally everyone was gone, all the dishes had been washed, and the inn was quiet, dark except for the flame glowing on the last candle in the dining room. Marina and Dan sat, a half-empty bottle of red wine between them, talking softly and enjoying the quiet.

"I'm so . . . impressed by all this," Dan said. "You really did the hard parts, you know. The plumbing and painting and plastering were without inspiration. But you turned it from a building into an inn."

She smiled. "And you like it, right? You don't think it's sickeningly quaint or anything?"

He looked puzzled. "It's beautiful. The room looks great—and just wait until you read Margo's review and you see what she said." He tilted his head. "Whatever gave you the idea it was sickeningly quaint?"

She took another sip of wine and then said, "Alex. He came up here. I didn't tell you about it, I guess because I wanted to try to figure it out for myself. But anyway, he hated what I've done." She sighed. "I guess I'm really hitting my head against the wall. But it just makes me feel very alone—and very sad—that he's so against what I'm doing, that we're so far apart. He's really the only family I have left."

Dan sighed. "I know. But I think you should realize something. He wouldn't be reacting so strongly in a negative way if there weren't another side of the

163

coin." He shrugged. "He's struggling inside right now, fighting with himself. And the winning side—the negative one—is the safe one to let out. But you know he loves you and that eventually it will all work out. I think you have to give him room, though. He needs time, Marina." He looked into her eyes and then away. And all at once she realized that what he had said about Alex's feelings was true of him as well.

"He feels the way you feel, in other words," she said, more forcefully than she had intended.

"I'm not sure I agree with that," Dan said, pouring himself some more wine.

She sighed. She didn't want to fight; not now; not when she was seeing Dan for the first time in so long. But she knew, too, that she had to speak, to voice feelings that would only grow if they were kept silent. For her life was at a turning point. It looked as if Windy Hill was going to do well, and she was truly on her own in a new and promising situation; now was the time to know where she stood. "I don't . . ." She sighed. "I don't want to fight, Dan. But I don't agree with what you're saying. The way you analyze my situation with Alex, it's as if I'm wrong to let him know what I want. And that's the way you seem to feel about our relationship, too." She paused, and he said nothing. "I'm so glad you're here. It's an important time for me. But part of this new phase I'm in—part of what I hope will be a new way of living for me—is knowing what I want, and then not getting stepped on or forgotten or ignored or a thousand other things because I'm either unaware or too scared to say anything.

"When we first started seeing each other, I had made a mistake—with Barclay. The kind I've been making my whole life. That situation was clear: he was married, and I don't want to go out with married men. I was disappointed—aside from finding out he was fairly obnoxious—because even though I hadn't been interested in marrying him, I had wanted the potential to be there." She sighed. "Because I'm at a point in my life when I just don't want to fool around. I don't want to have affairs that lead nowhere. I just . . . it's not fair to me. I've finally discovered I deserve better—and no one's out there looking to help me pick and choose; I've got to do it myself."

Dan sighed and looked into her eyes. When she met his deep brown gaze, she half-wished she had said nothing; for she wanted only to look into those eyes, so dark and affectionate, to reach out and hold his warm, strong hand. "You make it so difficult—" he began.

She shook her head. "Uh-uh. That's just not true, Dan. That's what I used to think, but I was wrong. Why do I deserve less?"

"I'm not saying you do," he cut in.

She looked at him steadily. "Then what are you saying?"

He sighed. "You're taking what I'm saying as if it's directed at you and you alone. I don't mean that, Marina. But for any person to expect any other person to be able to analyze his feelings and project the future at any given time is—"

"Oh come on," she interrupted. "We both know we're not talking about 'any given time.' This isn't a test, or a game. And anyway, I thought you were the one so given to projections of the future. What happened to your certainty about that?"

"I told you," he said gently. "Nothing has gone as I planned since I met you, Marina."

Softened by the affection in his voice, she looked into his eyes and for a few moments gazed at him in silence.

"Don't you see," she finally said. "I don't want to fight. I don't want to have a battle. But I don't want to have an endless affair, either, a relationship in which you basically live in New York and do your corporate law, and I live here and run a restaurant, and we see each other on weekends and make love and talk and pretend there's no issue hanging in the air."

He looked at her searchingly. "Are you always thinking about it?" he asked. "Are you always wondering where we're headed, whenever we talk, whenever we make love?"

"Of course not. But that doesn't mean it isn't important. Dan, I just can't . . . give myself to you— emotionally, physically, in every way I've been doing and loved doing—unless I know we're going somewhere. It's just too hard . . . in the end."

He sighed and took a sip of wine and then turned his dark eyes upon her. "Marina, I don't want to stop seeing you."

She was silent, waiting for more. But she waited, looking into his eyes, and nothing more came. "And?" she asked, annoyed. "And? But? What, Dan?"

He tiredly rubbed his fingers along the bridge of his nose and shook his head. "I don't want to stop seeing you. But I can't be unfair to you, either. I understand how you feel. And if I can't promise—"

She didn't want to hear any more. Suddenly she didn't even want to look at him anymore. Not if he was going to say he could promise nothing; not if this was the end. "Then go," she interrupted. She ignored the shock in his eyes and went on. "Please. I mean it. I don't want you here anymore."

He looked at her, his eyes dark with an expression she couldn't read, and then stood up. "Marina—"

"What?" she asked, her voice sharp.

He sighed and paused. "If you want to talk more, I'll be in town. Until midday."

Shocked, she forgot her anger for a moment. "In town? Why?"

He sighed. "It doesn't really matter now. Something I had been considering. But it's . . . it's over."

She tore away from his gaze. Somehow the fact that there was already a secret, something they didn't share, seemed fitting and horribly sad, sharpening their past full of sharing all the more. For a time they had had no secrets—only love. And it was over as suddenly as it had begun.

"Oh. I forgot," he said, reaching into his back pocket. "Here. You'll like this." He handed her a folded-up piece of paper.

When she unfolded it and saw what it was, she almost began to cry. It was the review Margo Fenning had written, entitled "Heaven on Earth," and somehow it seemed a reminder of everything she and Dan had shared, built together, loved.

"Well," Dan said. "I'll be at the motel in town until morning. You know where to reach me in the city after that."

She nodded, tears stealing her voice. She sat silently at the table as he went back into the bedroom—what had been "their" room—and then came out with his suitcase.

Their eyes met and held. And then he looked away.

Marina didn't watch as he walked the rest of the way through the dining room. She heard his footsteps as he walked through the commons room, remembered for a painful moment how they had once made love in that room, and then closed her eyes as she heard the door shut.

Marina didn't call him the next morning. What was there to say or do? They had gone as far as they were going to go, loved as much as they were going to love, cried out each other's names in need and satisfaction for the last time.

She wondered over and over again whether she had done the right thing, wondered whether she had spoken too soon or said too much. For she knew that if she had said nothing, Dan would have wanted to keep seeing her . . . perhaps forever.

But deep down she knew she had spoken the only

words she could have. For she couldn't have gone on with him in an affair forever, even if he could have. Not with the fear that there was no future except a repetition of the present, no future except something that he and he alone determined. But she wished there had been another way.

And she wished, against what she knew was her better judgment, that she had waited a little longer to speak the truth. For suddenly she felt utterly alone: the man she loved was gone; her family was gone except for one hostile brother she hardly knew anymore; and the world she had chosen rather precipitously to inhabit—a new life in a town in which she knew no one—made her feel more alone and vulnerable still.

When her two assistants showed up in the middle of the morning, Marina put on a show of confidence she didn't really feel but knew was necessary. After all, nothing in their world had changed, and there was no reason she had to let them know the pain she was feeling. Perhaps, too, if she acted as if nothing were wrong, she would soon feel that way as well.

The act did help. Judy and Lexie were still thrilled over the success of the evening before, and their pleasure in their work and in knowing their jobs were safe made them enthusiastic in a way that was contagious. As they came to Marina with ideas for further decorating, names of friends who might want to reserve the inn for private parties, and suggestions for dishes they wanted to try to learn to make on their own, Marina couldn't help getting caught up in their optimism.

During lunch, as Lexie, a pretty, dark-haired girl of sixteen, started running down a list of people she knew who were in some way connected with local papers, Marina thought of the review Margo Fenning had written. It lay folded on top of the bureau in her room, where she had put it unread after Dan had left. Last night she hadn't wanted to look at it, for she knew it would remind her of what she had had with Dan . . . and lost. But now she was ready—or would try to be—for all the good that could come into her life, and certainly ready for anything that might distract her.

"I have something I think will please you," she said, looking at Lexie and Judy. "I'll be right back."

The girls smiled and widened their eyes, and Marina laughed and went off to get the review. When she came back with it she sat down and raised her glass of Perrier in a toast. "To what I hope will be the first of lots of reviews to keep us happy and well known and in the black. Are you ready?"

"A review!" Lexie cried.

"In what?" Judy asked. "How come you didn't tell us?"

"I . . . didn't want to look at it quite yet," she said. "All right, here goes. It's from *East Side Living* magazine, and the review is titled 'Heaven on Earth.' "

"If French country dining in an isolated and breathtakingly beautiful section of the nearby countryside is your cup of tea, you are in for quite a brew indeed. Windy Hill, specializing in

170

French *cuisine minceur,* with an accent on fresh vegetables and herbs, is a jewel of a restaurant, the kind whose name and location I would be certain to keep for myself and my close friends if I weren't in the reviewing business.

"From the moment you arrive at the Windy Hill property, nestled in the rather spectacular-looking Shawangunk Mountains just below the Catskills, you know you are in for a treat for the soul as well as the palate. The air, the trees, the fragrances of herbs and the mountains seem magical even to the most jaded and urban of souls, and the magnificent job of restoration of the inn itself, still in progress, promises much for the future.

"Inside, the charm is everywhere, from the oak floors and solid, clean lines of the Shaker tables and chairs to the enchanting Laura Ashley curtains, tablecloths, and napkins. The help was harried but charming both nights I was there, and quite cheerful about explaining the various specials of the evening.

"And now, for the raison d'être of Windy Hill: to start, one can delight in fish pâté with herbs and greens, fruit and fresh mint compote, tomato and spinach tarts with thyme—all delicious and unbelievably fresh. Go on to breast of duckling with peppercorns, grilled fillet of beef with rosemary and garlic, or baked trout with dill and lemon, and you're sure to feel your life is complete. Untried (by me) but delicious-looking were stuffed chicken with tarragon, baked

171

scallops with lemon, and chicken mousse; I intend to return for these shortly. And as for desserts: amazingly, one can delight in a host of pleasures with a minimum of guilt: they are all, as desserts go, relatively unfattening, blasting the rule that says anything that good must be fattening, illegal, etc. etc. etc.: pears in red wine, hot peach tarts, baked bananas, light strawberry and orange custards are all out of this world; and if one's tastes run more to fruit and cheese, the former are fresh, the latter impeccably selected.

"I am told there are plans afoot to turn Windy Hill into a small inn as well, ultimately serving breakfast to guests only and dinners to guests and visitors. About these plans all I can say is that I for one was ready to move in last night, willing to sleep among boards and nails just to sample the fare once more. This after eating there twice in a row. Happily, though, the drive up from NYC along the Thruway is quick —about two hours; and if one is lucky enough to live closer, so much the better. Just remember it's only open Friday through Sunday at the moment. And if the restaurant gods continue to shed their very abundant grace upon Windy Hill as they have so far, it's a sure five-star entry for next year."

Marina smiled and put the review down on the table. "I don't believe it," she said quietly.

Judy laughed. "I've never been called harried but charming before. I think I like it."

"And cheerful," Lexie put in.

"Listen, you two, if any of the other reviews are even remotely as good as this one, we've really made it."

They sat in stunned silence for a few moments.

"Who was the woman who wrote it?" Judy asked. "Which one was she? We may have been harried, but I think I'd remember if you described her."

"Her name is Margo Fenning. She and her husband were here the first night. She has red hair and is about my age, very pretty, very lively, and her husband is kind of blond."

"Oh yeah," Lexie said. "Kind of blond and kind of cute. I remember. But they were here the second night with your friend. The one you, uh, seemed to know pretty well."

Marina smiled. "Yes. Well." She was about to say, That's all over now, but kept silent instead. No matter how much she liked her young helpers, they were neither her friends nor her confidantes, and in any event, she didn't want to talk about Dan at the moment. "Well," she said, setting her palms on the table. "Enough relaxation for the day. We'd better get back to work or there won't be any dinner tonight to be served by harried *or* unharried help."

And as she finished her coffee at the table, she realized it wasn't just time to get back to work; it was time to begin getting her life back in order. She had thought she had been on the road to independence, starting up Windy Hill and opening it on her own,

173

but now that Dan was gone, she realized all the work and hope and confidence had been tied up with him: the independence had been at least partially illusory.

Without giving herself enough time to talk herself out of it, she went back into her room and called Alex. For she suddenly realized that now was the perfect time—if there was going to be a perfect time —to try to resolve their problems or at least to begin to break through some of the barriers that had been separating them. She was feeling vulnerable and alone, and perhaps more ready than ever before to sit down and talk without arguing about Windy Hill or anything else; for when she had been saying that she wanted him to go in with her on the project, all she had meant, she realized, was that she wanted to be close.

"Hello," he said, his voice desultory.

"Alex, it's Marina."

He was silent. Then: "Look, I'm not feeling too well," he said quietly.

"What's the matter?" she asked, anxiety leaping into her voice.

"Oh, just a summer cold," he said, coughing into the phone.

"You sound awful. What if I come down and make you some soup?"

He was silent again.

"I mean it," she said. "It would help you, and we could talk." She paused. "Unless you have someone there taking care of you already."

He laughed—the first time she had heard him laugh in ages. "No, no such luck, sister dear. But why all this sibling concern all of a sudden? Windy Hill going downhill already?"

"The opposite, as a matter of fact. Read next week's *East Side Living* magazine and see. But thanks for thinking so much of me . . . brother dear." She closed her eyes, angry she had slipped back into the pattern they had both been trapped in for so long. "Sorry," she said. "Why don't I come down, then?"

"I don't understand," he said. "Marina, I've had dozens of colds before, and we've been out of touch for years. What gives?"

She sighed. "What gives is that I'm lonely," she said. "What gives is that I'm going to ignore the nonsense we put each other through because I think there's something really worthwhile to try for—some sort of . . . reconciliation, or understanding."

"Did Dan Sommers tell you that's what you should do?" he asked. "Get me on your side? Because there's something we haven't resolved, in case you've forgotten," he said. "But I guess that's why you're calling."

"What are you talking about?"

"The money from Windy Hill, Marina. I never thought there'd be any. But if there is, who gets it?"

She bit her lip. "You think that's why I'm calling?" she asked quietly.

"I don't know why you're calling," he said. "But I thought I'd throw out an educated guess."

"Well, you guessed wrong," she said. "It happens to belong to both of us. What I put in, I put in because I wanted to. If we sell, under one of the codicils to the will, we recoup according to what we

175

put in. But as you know, Alex, I don't plan to sell. However, I don't plan on calling you again, either. I called because I needed . . . I guess I needed a shoulder to cry on. Somehow I thought there was a chance it could be yours. But forget it. Good-bye, Alex."

She hung up and looked around at the bare walls of her room, feeling more alone than ever.

CHAPTER NINE

Marina found it almost impossible not to think about Dan; every room in the house reminded her of him; every special time of day—dawn, dusk, midnight— was a time they had made love, a time they had gazed into each other's eyes and held each other close.

Each time the phone rang—and now it rang often —she expected it to be him. For she had to admit that since he had first gone, she had not fully expected the separation to last. It wasn't as if she had been playing a game and he had called her bluff; she had never been more serious. But she had thought one of them would give in; she had thought even she might.

Yet she hadn't called him, and he hadn't called her.

Marina grew busier and busier every day as word of Windy Hill spread. She planted a small terraced vegetable garden along the slope and hired a boy part-time to do some of the heavy work around the inn and begin work on the upstairs rooms. And as each day passed she grew firmer in her commitment: she would remember the impetus that had led her to Windy Hill in the first place, and she would make it the guiding force behind every action she took. Her involvement with Dan had been so tied up with her feelings about Windy Hill that she had forgotten that initially Windy Hill had been a symbol of independence. And it would be that once more. She had left the city, in part, to get away from relationships that led nowhere and a job that was unrewarding. She owed it to herself to make the move more rewarding than she had even dreamed.

One afternoon about two weeks after Dan had left, Margo Fenning showed up unexpectedly. Marina, Judy, and Lexie were chopping vegetables around the large table in the middle of the kitchen when Marina heard footsteps clacking across the wood floors of the commons room, and then a vaguely familiar female "Hello?"

"In here," Marina called, standing up and wiping her hands on her apron. She was surprised when she saw it was Margo; she hadn't expected to see her again for months, as her reviewing took almost all her time. "What a surprise," Marina said. "And a nice one."

Margo smiled. "I can only stay for a few minutes," she said. "I'm off to Hyde Park to the Culinary Institute. But I wanted to stop in and see how things were going."

"Great. Busy, as you can see," Marina said, nodding at the piles of chopped vegetables on the table. "Thanks in no small measure to you," she added. "I'd say we're running about eighty percent local and twenty percent city customers right now, which probably means twenty percent from you."

Margo's eyes sparkled. "You don't know what you have here," she said. "Your next problem is going to be how to turn the crowds away."

Marina laughed. "Come on out to the dining room for a glass of wine," she said.

A few moments later they were sitting in two of the quilted easy chairs Marina had just bought for the far end of the dining room as a small sitting area that could be used during the day in addition to the commons room. The view was lovely looking out across the lawn, and the setting sun was just visible through the trees edging the creek.

"So tell me," Margo said. "How is Dan taking all this wild success?"

Marina sighed. "I, uh, don't know," she said quietly and took a sip of wine. She answered the look of surprise in Margo's eyes by adding, "We broke up . . . let's see . . . three weeks ago, just about."

"I'm stunned," Margo said quietly. "Really stunned. The way he was talking, I would have thought you two would be married by now and that he would have opened an office in town." She paused. "I'm sorry, Marina. Really. And very surprised." She raised a brow. "You did know about the office, didn't you? You turned rather pale just now when I mentioned it."

Marina shook her head. "I didn't know, no. You don't mean that he opened one—"

"No, no. But he was thinking of it—talking about how you were so smart and had done the right thing leaving the city and doing what you really wanted."

"Yes. Well. It didn't quite—it just didn't work out," she said vaguely, lost in thought.

Margo didn't stay much longer. She sampled some of Marina's tarte maison, picked a few herbs from the garden, and apologized at least half a dozen times for having pried. And then she left, advising Marina that she would get over Dan more quickly than she might expect.

Marina was slightly annoyed at Margo's last piece of advice but more annoyed still at herself: did she show her feelings so clearly, even to near-strangers?

More than anything else, though, she was confused by what Margo had told her. If Dan had been planning to rent an office up in the mountains—even if he had just been considering it—what did it mean?

For the rest of the afternoon questions about Dan kept coming to her, making her lose track of the work she was doing. She thought of calling him, as she had considered for days. But she knew that she had in the long run acted wisely, and that if she called him there was a chance she would turn back to him at any moment, throwing away all her resolves.

And so she didn't call, that day or the next. She was meeting new people gradually, in town and at the restaurant, and for the first time since she had arrived she felt truly confident that she could make a new life for herself in the mountains, one in which she wouldn't be isolated in her work but happy in every area of her life. She knew it would take time, but she saw that it was possible and was looking forward to the challenge and adventure of it all.

On the next Wednesday morning, just as she was sleepily going over some marketing lists at dawn, she heard the sound of a car motor. She looked at her watch and saw it was only 5:30 and, somewhat alarmed, ran to the commons room and looked through the windows.

It was Alex's car. Mystified, she ran out to meet him.

He got out of the car slowly, stood up, and rubbed his temples as if in pain. Yet when he looked at Marina out of the corner of his eye, he was almost smiling, as if with a pleasant secret. "Surprised?" he asked, a corner of his mouth going up.

"Very. I wasn't planning on seeing or speaking to you for a long time."

He grimaced. "I can imagine. Do you have any aspirins, by the way?"

She nodded. "Sure. Come on in."

He began walking up the driveway with her toward the inn, then stopped and took a deep breath. "Smells just the same as it did fifteen years ago, doesn't it?"

She smiled. "Mm, it's great. Come on in."

A few minutes later, after Marina had made coffee and Alex had taken some aspirin, they sat at the kitchen table in the gray light of the dawn.

"Listen," Alex said. "Sorry about how early it is.

181

I had thought you'd be asleep and I'd just sit outside." He sighed. "I was out late drinking, thinking about what I had said to you last week, thinking about something Dan had said, and I just had to come."

She looked up from her coffee. "When did you talk to Dan?" she asked.

He frowned. "Yesterday. I called to ask him about the memoirs and albums Tatiana had left. He said he still had them—that he had meant to give them to you." He looked into her eyes. "Marina, I didn't know you and Dan Sommers had been seeing each other."

She nodded. She wanted to ask Alex how Dan had sounded, but she hesitated. She didn't want to expose her feelings as she had to Margo Fenning—at least not yet.

"Did you break the relationship off?" Alex asked. "It kind of sounded that way to me."

"Why?" she asked.

Alex shrugged. "He sounded depressed, and—well, for one thing, he really lit into me about that 'sickeningly quaint' comment I made." He smiled crookedly. "Words I should have known I'd live to regret. He was really angry and called me a few names I won't repeat."

Marina smiled. "Good. Because you deserved it, you know."

Alex looked into her eyes. "I'm sorry," he said. "I said a lot of things I didn't mean." He sighed. "I guess Windy Hill really brought out a lot of competitiveness in me that I haven't felt so directly in years."

She frowned. "But why?"

Alex shrugged. "The most common reason in the world—the same reason we competed like hell against each other all our lives: for love from Mom and Dad, and then Tatiana." He smiled. "Even after she was gone."

Marina sighed. "I didn't mean to take Windy Hill from you—or to beat you to it, either. It just seemed that way, I guess." She paused. "You can still—"

"No," he interrupted. "At some level I'd like to help—maybe later on. But you took the risks, Marina. It isn't my kind of thing, anyway. And something Dan said made me realize it's better for me to leave you alone for a while."

"What did he say?" she asked.

"Well, it was when he really lit into me for criticizing what you had done. And he said you were the only one of the three of us who was willing to take a risk for something you believed in, and that I didn't deserve to be associated with Windy Hill in any way."

Marina frowned. "He didn't have a right to say that to you. Windy Hill is half yours."

"But you're the one who's done something with it. Listen—I'm not going to refuse any profits that come my way. I could really use the money. But I think I'm going to try to pull my own company up by its bootstraps if I can and concentrate on it for a while, the way you did with Windy Hill."

Marina smiled. "Sounds good to me. But tell me, how did your conversation with Dan end up? Was he still angry?"

Alex shrugged. "Neutral, I'd say. He was certainly calmer and more polite than when I first called. He seemed really preoccupied by the end." Alex looked at her carefully. "And he asked all about you. If you ask me, Marina, you look as interested as he sounded. I think you should call him."

She smiled. "Why would I ask you? I've hardly spoken to you in years."

He looked hurt by her words, but then she said, "I'm only kidding," and he smiled.

For the rest of the morning, as she and Alex explored all their old haunts on the property, her mind was on Dan. Now more than ever before she deeply wanted to call, even just to hear his voice and talk. She had always hated the fact that after her divorce, she had stopped speaking to Rick altogether. How could it be that two people who had been married—two people who had thought they were in love—could drift so far apart? It was as if the marriage had never existed. And she didn't want the same thing to happen with Dan. Her relationship with him deserved better.

Yet she knew they couldn't just be friends; they couldn't go back.

Alex left that afternoon, after having lunch with Marina and promising to come back for a visit soon. After he left, Marina felt wonderful; now she had a relationship—the beginnings of one, at least—with her brother after years of estrangement.

She hummed as she cleared the lunch dishes; she felt better than she had in weeks. And later on, as the sun was setting, when she heard a car in the driveway she walked out to the commons room with a spring in her step, in a perfect mood to meet with anyone who wanted to look around and find out what nights Windy Hill served dinner.

But when she stepped out onto the veranda, she saw that it was Dan who had come. He was walking toward her, in a red polo shirt and faded jeans, his eyes looking into hers with a mixture of uncertainty and sure affection.

Unwilling to trust her responses, she stayed on the veranda.

He looked very tanned—much more than when she had last seen him—and his dark hair had blondish highlights from the sun.

He came up the steps and stood close but not touching, at a distance they hadn't tested since their first night together. His eyes were beautiful, and she wanted to take him in her arms, but she didn't move.

"I had to come," he said quietly. "I didn't want to call and hear you say no, and I had to talk." He reached out and rested his palm against her cheek, and involuntarily her hand came up and covered his. She closed her eyes and inhaled the scent she had missed so much, brushed her lips across the warm hand she loved, forgot herself completely until suddenly she tensed and opened her eyes, realizing she had let herself go in a way she hadn't meant to at all. She was about to take his hand away. But she looked into his eyes, and her lips parted; and with a moan he pulled her to him and covered her mouth with his. Warmth, desire, love, tears brimmed as she wrapped her arms around him and tasted the sweetness of his mouth with the deepest love she had ever felt.

He pulled away and stroked her hair back from her face. "How I ever could have left you," he murmured. "I was so blind. And so unhappy." He leaned down and brushed his lips across her forehead. "I had been trying to force myself to forget about you." He smiled. "I wasn't succeeding, but I was trying. And then your brother called me—about Tatiana's memoirs and photographs, of all things. I was letting him have it about all sorts of issues, and I caught myself: I heard what was in my voice—a passion that had little to do with what I was saying and everything to do with how I felt about you. I hardly remember the rest of my conversation with Alex. All I knew at that moment was that I had to see you."

She looked into his eyes. "I wanted to call you," she said quietly. "But I didn't want to get caught up again, Dan. Not if—"

"Shh," he said softly, covering her lips with his for a brief moment. "Don't worry about ifs," he murmured. "That's what I realized I had to stop doing. I had to forget about complications and maybes and what ifs and pay attention to the one truth I know—that I love you, Marina."

"Oh, Dan," she said, looking into his deep brown eyes so clear with love.

"I had known it before, and run from it before: I had even looked into opening an office up here." He smiled. "But there was a little too much commitment in something like that." He sighed. "When I went back to New York I made a hundred-and-eighty-degree turn back to what I had been. I went out to the Hamptons for weekends and had a rotten time, I continued to work on the Texas case—the one I disliked so much—and realized I was keeping my views to myself just to keep things going smoothly at the office. As each day passed part of me knew I was going in the wrong direction, running from the only woman I've ever really loved, and from the kind of life I want to lead: running my own office, choosing clients I believe in helping, doing exactly what I set out to do at the beginning but lost sight of somewhere along the way." He gazed into her eyes. "Marina, I love you. I've taken so long to say it that now I want to say it every moment, every time I look into your eyes."

She smiled. "I love you too," she said.

"I don't know how I ever could have let you go, darling. But now that I'm here, I don't ever want to leave again."

"Then stay," she whispered.

He smiled. "I'll stay on one condition."

She looked up at him questioningly, one side of her mouth turned up in a smile. "Just what condition is that?"

"That you marry me," he said softly.

She hugged him and then looked into his eyes. "I'd love to so much."

His eyes shined with pleasure. "I don't know if it's going to work in every single way—if I'm going to be able to find enough work up here, or even like being up here all the time. But I know one thing—

we'll make it work. And nothing is as important as our being together."

She smiled. "I love you," she whispered, and he gathered her into his arms.

He carried her into her room—"their" room once again—and they were together once more, undressing quickly, holding each other close, drawing back and gazing at each other with pure, deep love.

Marina had missed him physically as well as emotionally, and as his hands cupped her breasts and his mouth closed over a nipple, she responded with explosive need, holding him tightly against her and kneading his firm flesh with passion.

"Darling," he whispered, his warm hands braced at either side of her, his hard frame insisting against her as she arched in desire. "Darling, I want you to be mine forever," he whispered huskily. And with a thrilling surge he made them one and set a sure rhythm and motion that came from love, knowledge of her needs, hunger for her pleasure. They were forceful, hungry, passionate as they told each other through whispers, breaths, moans, sheer pleasure, and shimmering release that their love was deep, endless, forever.

Afterward they lay there entwined, looking into each other's eyes, each wondering how separation had been possible, each wondering how doubts had existed.

"I love you," she whispered, resting her head in the curve of his shoulder.

She felt him smile. "I love you more," he said.

She propped herself up and grinned as she looked at him. "Nope. Not possible."

He laughed and slid a warm hand along her back. "We'll see about that." And then his smile faded almost imperceptibly. "I just thought of something."

She frowned. "What?"

"Nothing bad. Just odd. Something I had forgotten for weeks. Remember what Tatiana wrote—that if you could ever find a place like Windy Hill, to hold onto it no matter what?"

Marina nodded.

"Well, remember she kept the place a secret all those years? You thought she had sold it, but she hadn't."

"That's right. And you never told me why she had kept it a secret."

Dan smiled. "I had my reasons. But at this point I guess I don't have to worry about ruining my image as a hardheaded lawyer." He caressed her cheek. "You already know I'm an incurable romantic. And so was Tatiana, Marina. She didn't want anyone to know about Windy Hill because she believed it was enchanted—endowed with the power to create love as she had known it. And she wanted to be sure to give that love to the right people at the right time, without pressure from anyone—including other relatives—who would want Windy Hill for the future. She had thought it could help you and Alex resolve your problems"—he smiled—"but if she's out there somewhere, she knows her calculations were a bit off."

Marina smiled. "I wonder—because she wanted

you to read the memoirs, after all. She had you involved from the start." Marina paused. "You don't . . . do you believe all of that, Dan? About the enchantment?"

He slowly shook his head. "But I know one thing for certain. I would have fallen under your spell wherever we had met, and wherever we had gone. And I'll be under your spell and in love with you forever, Marina."

"Oh, Dan, I love you so much," she whispered. And as he took her into his arms and once again showed her how very deeply he loved her, the magic was within them both.

LOOK FOR NEXT MONTH'S
CANDLELIGHT ECSTASY ROMANCES ®

When You Want A Little More Than Romance—

Try A Candlelight Ecstasy!